TROUBLE AT BETTS PETS

 Kelly Easton

CANDLEWICK PRESS
CAMBRIDGE, MASSACHUSETTS

Copyright © 2002 by Kelly Easton

First edition 2002

Library of Congress Cataloging-in-Publication Data

Easton, Kelly.
Trouble at Betts Pets / Kelly Easton. — 1st ed.
p.   cm.
Summary: A number of changes are taking place in fifth-grader Aaron's life: business at the family pet shop is declining, forcing his parents to consider selling the store; luxury condominiums are going up on the land that houses a community garden, displacing the eccentric old woman who resides there; and Aaron gets to know his seemingly perfect classmate Sharon when she begins to tutor him in math.
ISBN 0-7636-1580-3
[1. Pet shops — Fiction. 2. Homeless persons — Fiction. 3. Schools — Fiction. 4. Friendship — Fiction.] I. Title.
PZ7.E13155 Tr 2002
[Fic] — dc21   2001035064

2 4 6 8 10 9 7 5 3 1

Printed in the United States of America

This book was typeset in Goudy.

Candlewick Press
2067 Massachusetts Avenue
Cambridge, Massachusetts 02140

visit us at www.candlewick.com

For my mom.
And for my favorite children, Isabelle and Isaac Easton Spivack,
David Kline, Celia and Katie Easton Wickham, Katie Sidders;
and the big ones, Jeff, Eric, and Gabrielle Easton.

ACKNOWLEDGMENTS

And always, thanks to my husband, Arthur Jay Spivack, for all of
his help, to Randi Easton Wickham for being my first reader,
to Deborah Wayshak and Liz Bicknell of Candlewick Press for
their wonderful suggestions, to copyeditor Karen Weller-Watson,
and to Jane Dystel.

chapter 1

I had just finished the face on the rhesus monkey. He was standing in a clearing, underneath a eucalyptus tree. His head was tilted up like he was looking at something in the sky.

The difficult part, when I'm drawing a person or an animal, is the eyes. Most of the personality is reflected in these two small organs.

My monkey's expression still looked blank. I took my eraser and etched out a tiny triangle in the pupil of one eye. It added a brightness, a spark. I was just doing the same on the other eye when Mrs. Felty, my fifth-grade teacher, sauntered over. (Did I mention that I was *supposed* to be doing math?)

"Some people have brains that think from the left side; some from the right. I read this" — Mrs. Felty leaned against my desk — "in *Psychology Today*."

Mrs. Felty attempted a smile. Her tongue flicked against her lips. Have you ever seen a gecko? It's a type of reptile. Mrs. Felty is a dead ringer for one. She's kind of scaly and beige. She can be stone still for an incredibly long time. Then she moves very suddenly, in small jerks.

Don't get me wrong; she's not all that bad. It's just, she's so sweet and helpful, she's like having a bad toothache and no aspirin in sight.

My name is Aaron Betts and I grew up in a pet store. I wasn't kept in a cage, or anything. And I've actually never *lived* in the shop. But close enough. My parents are the proud owners of Betts Pets. For as long as I can remember, I've spent every weekend, afternoon, and most evenings cleaning hamster cages, feeding fish, washing reptiles, training birds, and playing with bunnies, kittens, and puppies.

Because of this, I have a problem: I think of people as animals. My mom, for example, is a canary. She flutters around the store, from task to task, and chirps at the customers as they tell her long stories about their cat's new litter box or their turtle's shell fungus. The way some people are about pets, you'd think they were talking about their babies.

My dad is like a basset hound. He's six feet two and weighs about 270 pounds. He's got great big brown droopy eyes, and he moves about as slowly as my mom does quickly. Basset hound puppies are the cutest things you can imagine. You've probably seen them in shoe commercials. They've got long floppy ears and big sad faces. We sell a ton of them at Christmas, but half of them get returned. Why? Bassets have a stubborn streak. It's impossible to keep them off of the furniture. And they don't housebreak well. They'd just as soon pee right on the couch as have to walk all the way outside, where it might be cold and uncomfortable.

Of course, my dad doesn't pee on the couch, or anything like that. He's just very slow moving and sort of stubborn. And his idea of fun is curling up in some comfortable spot and falling asleep. A couple of years ago, my mom made him go to the doctor. They put him in some fancy sleep laboratory, attached wires to his head, followed the flickers of his rapid eye movement, the brain patterns of his dreams. Diagnosis: sleep apnea and narcolepsy. Sleep apnea is where you snore a lot, and stop breathing sometimes, during sleep. Narcolepsy is where you just drop off to sleep at strange moments. Like, he'll fall asleep sitting on a stool at the desk. One time he flopped right onto the cash register, making the money drawer fly open. "Sale!" Mom yelled across the store.

The doctor gave him some pills and some things to put on his nose, but he still falls asleep at odd times.

So the old saying that opposites attract seems to be true in the case of my parents. But they get along pretty well, probably because they both love animals.

Betts Pets has been owned by three generations of Bettses. My mom met my dad when she was in high school and came to work at the shop part-time. During college, she kept working nights and weekends, and when she graduated with her teaching certificate, instead of going into the classroom, she started working days. As my dad says, what else could they do but get married?

Mrs. Felty tapped the drawing, which I'd tried to slide under my math work. I started, and the class laughed.

"Some people are good at art." She held my drawing up to the class. "Some are good at math!" She nodded toward Sharon Trout. (Despite her fish name, Sharon Trout is a Siamese cat: spoiled, snobby, pretty in a kind of overly prissy way. She's a straight-A student who spends her summers in places like France and the Hamptons.) "What I have decided, then, is that I will pair up different sides of the brain to make one unified whole. Aaron"—Felty tapped my desk—"Sharon will tutor you in math. Tracy, Steven will tutor you in grammar."

It was the usual trick—Mrs. Felty's attempt to make those of us who were failing a subject feel good, while embarrassing us in front of the whole class. I noticed that she didn't mention me tutoring Sharon in art.

The list continued, but I didn't listen anymore. Sharon Trout nodded at me like a queen to a servant. *Meow*, I could practically hear her say. Did she have bells on her little collar to scare the birds away?

I looked down at my math sheet. What I'd sort of understood a few minutes ago now looked like hieroglyphics. We'd studied those in social studies last year—the ancient linguistic system using pictures. Now *those* were interesting.

The bell rang. My best friend, Tony Wong, pulled on his baseball glove as he ran out of the room. "Hey," he whispered, "Sharon and Aaron; they rhyme."

He could joke about it. He got to go out and play while I would do my chores, then study.

I felt Sharon's paw on my shoulder. "We need to make an appointment for me to help you," she purred. "I have an opening in my schedule today, because my viola lesson was canceled."

An opening in her schedule?

"Okay." I didn't know what else to say.

"Where shall we meet?" she asked. "I'm not allowed to have guests at my house because my mother is away."

"Mine, I guess."

"Your address?"

"Twenty ninety-four Chestnut."

"Where's that?"

"Just past the old Riggs Apartments."

"Where all those drunks and gangs hang out?"

"Yeah," I said, enjoying her nervous look.

"If I must, I must," she agreed. "Four o'clock."

chapter 2

Every day since kindergarten, I've counted the steps from school to the pet shop. It always takes 264 steps to get from the door of Myrtle Elementary to Betts Pets.

Even though I've gotten bigger, the number of steps has remained the same. Why? Because I keep it that way. When I was little, I took huge strides, carefully avoiding all cracks that would break my mom's back. Now, I just take smaller and smaller steps. I guess I like consistency. If that isn't math, what is?

The steps are the only things that have stayed the same, though. When I started elementary school, I walked past Riggs Apartments. It was a nice apartment complex, seven stories high. On the first floor, there were shops: a bakery and grocer's, a dry cleaner's, a florist's, a coffee shop. A doorman in a green-and-gold uniform waved at everyone who walked by. Dogs walked their owners. Ladies carried grocery bags. Kids bounced balls or wrote with chalk on the sidewalk.

Two years ago, though, the building burned down. The remains were condemned. My dad and I stood on the sidewalk across the street and watched a great big wrecking ball swing into what was left of the building.

Now, as far as businesses go, there's only us and Wong's, the Chinese take-out where we often get our meals.

For a while, the lot was empty. Now, there are the beginnings of a new building: steel beams rising from the dirt, like the skeleton of a dinosaur. The structure for the new apartments seemed to appear overnight, but then, something went wrong. Dad read in the paper that the company that owned the land had gone bankrupt and the city planned to put in a housing project.

Last summer, people started hanging out on the land. At first, it was just a few guys drinking out of paper bags, and a couple of men with shopping carts full of cans.

Then, a bunch of people from a nearby housing project came and dug out a big plot on the land. Where there had been only dirt and rocks, the people planted vegetables and flowers. I watched the tiny plants grow tall and blossom until the garden looked like someone had tossed a piece of paradise from the window.

The gardeners are all shapes and sizes, and most of them come and go, but one old lady, Bertha, is there every day.

Bertha always wears the same green shaggy coat, gray pants, ski cap, and little beat-up boots, with tattered fur at the edges, that look like bedroom slippers. In summer, she was usually on her hands and knees pulling weeds, sprinkling fertilizer, picking vegetables and loading them into a wicker basket. Once, I saw her catch a butterfly on her finger and just stare at it for a long time.

Now, in winter, she sits on a folding chair, with her empty basket. Most of the time, she's alone. Maybe she's guarding the plot or something, or maybe she just likes to watch the crows that hang out there waiting for someone to throw them a crumb.

At any rate, she's definitely on her own invisible planet, because each day, she greets me with a different little speech. Most of what she says has to do with nursery rhymes. "Someone is throwing the starlight, star bright from the sky, Captain," she'll say, "but who will catch it?"

She calls me Captain, and I know her name is Bertha, because she always tells me. "If this little piggy went to the market, why didn't the others go to Florida? The piggy promised me roast beef, and then I had none. My name is Bertha."

Bertha kind of gives me a kick, but I feel sad for her. One time when I had a dollar in my pocket, from winning a bet with Tony Wong, I gave it to her. I thought she could buy a cup of coffee or maybe a clean pair of socks, but she just looked at the money, held it up to the light, and handed it back to me. "No good," she said. "Pyramid power is gone. And in God we don't trust." It made me feel pretty bad when she said that, because I could see life hadn't given her a good deal.

Once, I asked my mom if Bertha had anywhere to live.

"I'm sure she does." Mom shuddered. "Let's hope she does."

I'd looked at the puppies in their big pen, all curled up together. We take good care of our pets and have a good reputation; that's why we're still open even though our part of Cleveland has gone sour. I thought about how a rich lady will come in and buy a Pekingese. She'll keep him in a little dog bed and dress him up in a coat, buy him the expensive canned food or just feed him right from the table. "People treat their animals better than each other," my dad once joked, but maybe he was right.

Today, Bertha was in her usual place, at step 160, huddled in her chair against the cold. She stood up, and I waited for her to give her speech. "Peas porridge hot. Peas porridge, why bother to put peas in porridge when peas taste nasty and the cow who jumped over the moon got far enough from gravity to float away. It's magnetism, you know. Animal magnetism."

I waited a minute to see that she was finished. She always seems satisfied when she's finished her speech.

"My name is Bertha," she said. Then she sat back down on her folding chair.

"Good story," I said. "See you later."

"Bye, Captain. Don't forget to write."

chapter 3

The first thing I do when I walk into the shop is take off my coat. I always empty out the pockets, hang it on the lowest rung of the coat rack, then spin the rack on its stand. "Ritualistic children are *usually* good in math," Mrs. Felty had told my dad at a parent-teacher conference. It must be something she read in that magazine, but my dad had looked as puzzled as I felt. "Aaron's great at math," my dad said. "He's been working the cash register since he was five."

"But there's more to math than dollars and cents. There's fractions — and trigonometry. There's algebra."

At that moment, Dad had one of his attacks and fell fast asleep. His snoring sounded like a train whistle. "Mr. Betts?" Felty tapped him on the arm.

Sometimes I think my dad's narcolepsy is pretty convenient.

The second thing I do is say hi to each and every animal. When I was three or four, I would *shout* my greetings, much to the customers' amusement. I name every animal that arrives, no matter how short its stay: "Hi, Fluffy! Hi, Dover! Hi, Jake!" Mom says there were people from the neighborhood who actually made it a point to stop in and watch my act.

I still say hi to them, but silently. And if it's busy and I don't get a chance to greet them, I feel really unsettled.

See, it's true — what Mrs. Felty said. I do have certain habits — rituals — and I don't like to change them. Like, after school, I always have five cheese won tons, a glass of milk, and a fortune cookie — and I don't read the fortune until I've cleared my place, thrown away the wrapper, and eaten the cookie. Lately, Wong's has changed fortune cookie companies. It used to be that I could open my cookie and be told that I was destined for greatness in the world: YOU WILL BE RICH AND FAMOUS, YOUR TALENTS WILL WIN YOU MANY FRIENDS, THE NOBEL PRIZE IS YOURS FOR THE TAKING.

Now, the fortunes are filled with little moral scoldings: HE WHO TRAVELS TOO FAST GETS NOWHERE, SHE WHO EATS MOST SUFFERS INDIGESTION, WORK IS ITS OWN REWARD, that kind of stuff. Nothing to get excited about.

Tony tells me his dad says he has received lots of complaints about the new fortunes but that the cookies taste better. What does taste have to do with fortune cookies?

I finished my chores and snack. Then I cracked open the cookie and put the dry, hard pieces in my mouth, waited for them to soften, chewed, and swallowed. I unrolled the little paper. WHEN LIFE GIVES YOU LEMONS, MAKE LEMONADE, it read. At that moment, I heard the little chime on the door ring, and I knew it was her — Sharon. She was a lemon all right, and I've never liked lemonade.

chapter 4

"This is your *house?*" Sharon asked. Most kids think it's cool to own a pet shop, but sometimes I get tired of it. There are endless chores, for one thing, and sometimes I'd rather be out playing baseball or ice hockey, or whatever other game Tony's playing.

"Duh. This is my *shop.*"

"It stinks in here." Sharon held her upturned nose.

"It's the pets." I shrugged.

"My pet doesn't smell like that."

"And what is your pet?"

"A dalmatian."

"What's her name?"

"Spot," she said, "and it's a him."

Spot! Very original.

"How's his hearing?" I asked.

"Okay, I guess."

"Because one-third of all dalmatians are born deaf and have to be destroyed, and one-third are born half deaf. They also have to drink lots of water because they often have problems with their urinary tracts."

"Gross. Do I *need* to know about this?"

"If you own one, you do," I scolded.

"Whatever," she said, unimpressed with my ample knowledge. "Phew! How can you stand smelling this all the time?"

"Believe me, if you had two hundred and sixty-four animals, instead of one dalmatian, your house would smell like this."

"Where're the puppies?"

"We sold out of them for Christmas, and people usually don't buy again until spring. It's a seasonal thing."

She walked slowly around the shop, her face all scrunched up like a raisin.

"Eww. What are those?"

"What, the fish?"

"It's like you can see through them. Are those their intestines?"

"Guppies. They're pretty cool, but ordinary. Now if you want to see something special . . ."

I was going to show her the angelfish. My dad got it as a gift from an old lady who had run a pet store downtown. He'd helped her out a lot after her husband died, and when she went out of business, she gave him this rare angelfish, an iguana, the myna bird, and a batch of bunnies we sold last Easter. The angelfish is the most beautiful fish I've ever seen. My dad would like to keep the animals, but Mom likes to point out that we could use the money. I overheard my parents talking the other night: "If we didn't own the building outright," my mom said, "we'd be out of business."

Before I could show Sharon, she ran past me and stopped at the hamsters. "They're dead!" She sounded pretty freaked out. "In a pile."

"They're just sleeping. They're nocturnal. They get really active at night."

"I *know* what *nocturnal* means!"

Her exclamation had roused my dad from his snooze. He perked his ears and strolled over. "Who's the girl?" he asked me as if she were invisible.

"Dad, this is Sharon Trout. She's tutoring me in math."

"I knew a Trout once. He was a sanitary engineer. Used to play cards at the Lions Club. Any relation?"

"My dad is a psychiatrist," she said. "Not a trash man."

"A head shrinker, eh?"

"We'd better study now, Dad."

My dad fixed his hound's eyes on Sharon. I could tell he didn't like what he saw. "That real fur?"

"Uh . . ." Sharon touched her coat nervously. "Chinchilla."

"Ya know how they kill those poor little animals? First they put 'em in a vise. They're wide-awake, mind you. No anesthesia . . ." He started his tirade. Both my parents are vegetarians and feel pretty strongly about how animals are treated in research and stuff like that. Neither of them would touch a fur coat to save their lives. Fortunately, when Mom noticed that Dad was awake, she flew over. "The filter on the big aquarium's out," she ordered. "The myna bird needs his lesson, and someone's got to do something about Twinkle-doon . . ."

"Okay. Okay." Dad pointed to Sharon. "Chinchilla," he sneered.

Mom winced, but she has better manners. "Is this a new friend, Aaron? How nice! Make sure you offer her some won ton."

"Okay."

I know that everyone my age is embarrassed by their parents, but you've got to agree mine take the cake.

"Won ton?" I offered.

"Yech," she said.

"Milk?"

"Let's get down to work," Sharon snapped. "My chauffeur is picking me up at five sharp."

"You have a chauffeur?"

"Only when my mom's away. She's at a golf tournament in North Carolina. She's a pro."

"Oh."

"Where do you . . . uh . . . study?" She peered around the shop.

"I really don't need help with my math. I just haven't been that interested lately."

"Right!"

"Well, maybe a little with the fractions."

"Is there somewhere we can go that doesn't stink?"

"The supply room."

"What's that?"

"That's where we keep all the pet food and stuff. It's back here."

We walked into the storeroom. I go there whenever I want to be alone or do my homework. It's a small windowless room filled with shelves of dog food, birdseed, and chew toys and stuff. In the middle is a big card table, above which hangs a light bulb. To Sharon, I'm sure it was as dumpy as anything, but it was my sanctuary. When I was little, I would make forts out of empty boxes, hang a blanket in the entrance, and imagine I was on safari or in the trenches or flying a plane. Now, when I have a good book and need some peace and quiet, or I want to concentrate on a drawing, I go there.

"I guess we'll have to work here." Sharon plopped down at the table. She opened the book. "Okay, the trick to algebra is in deciphering the code. Pretend you're a detective on a mystery and you've . . . What's that noise?"

"What noise?"

"It's like a whisper . . . or a song?"

"I don't hear anything."

"Singing."

"It's probably one of the birds."

"But it's coming from back there."

"What have you got? Superhuman hearing?"

"Or above? What's up there?"

"Air."

"Right above!"

"Just an empty apartment. Nothing."

"Why is it empty?" She was a regular cross-examiner.

"We just put old boxes there and stuff. It's really tiny."

"Well, whatever. So you're a detective and you have to break the code . . ."

It's funny, but lately, I've been hearing sounds, too. Sometimes I imagine I hear voices. Other times I just hear a scratchy, skittering sound. Frankly, I think we may have rats, but I didn't want to mention that to Sharon. It was clear that she looked down on me plenty as it was; not that I cared.

"No matter how complicated the problem," Sharon instructed, "you have to start with the lowest common denominator."

I leaned over my math homework and tried to concentrate, but my mind kept wandering off. For me, numbers are codes to a million different daydreams.

"Okay, here's the remainder," Sharon said, and I thought about what it would be like to be on safari. I

thought about Dr. Leakey, who started an elephant preserve in Africa. Poachers will slaughter a pack of elephants and gouge out their tusks just for a few pounds of
ivory. Leakey's preserve saved hundreds of elephants.

"And x in this case," Sharon said, "is equal to one-
eighth."

I thought about the time that we took a vacation on a
ranch in Texas. The lady who ran it taught me how to
ride a horse, and how to make a big lasso out of a rope
and swing it over a pole. The lady said I was a natural
cowboy. That's what I want: to work with animals, but
outdoors, maybe in some strange country.

"And x in this one . . ."

Then my thoughts shifted to Bertha, for some reason.
She must have been a kid once and had parents. She
must have studied math.

"Are you paying attention?" Sharon socked me on
the arm.

My elbow went right out from under me. "Huh?"

"What did I just say?"

"x equals one-fourth?"

"Mrs. Felty was being kind when she said you use one
side of your brain. I don't think you're using any brain
at all."

I considered asking Sharon where she went to charm school or why her braces looked like the barbed wire at a high-security prison, but I was saved from being rude by my mom. She tapped on the door and peered in. "Aaron, I'm sorry to interrupt, but did you sell a mouse?"

"No."

"You're sure? Because I'm definitely missing a mouse."

"Which one?"

"Um. I think it's Ronald Reagan. Either that, or Slalom. I can't tell them apart."

"Slalom has a gray streak on his chest. That's how you tell them apart."

"You didn't sell one?"

"No. I'd remember if I did."

"And last week, two of the goldfish disappeared."

"They probably died," Sharon piped up. "Every time I've bought a goldfish from a pet store, it's died in two days."

"You must've overfed it," Mom replied primly.

"My mom made me flush so many down the toilet that she said it was grossing her out and she wouldn't buy me any more."

"If any pet had died, I would know," Mom scolded.

"Did you ask Dad?" I suggested.

"Yes, and he said he didn't sell anything but some cat food."

"I heard that mice will eat their offspring when they're born," Sharon offered. She's one of those kids who has something to say about everything, a real authority.

"My mice do not eat each other!" Mom replied indignantly. "Could someone have stolen him?"

"Why would someone *steal* a mouse?" Sharon seemed to have no clue how much she was irritating my mom.

"Well . . ." Mom absently wiped a crumb off the table. "If you liked mice . . . or . . ."

"To feed a snake." I finished her sentence.

Sharon Trout crinkled up her nose. "Yech!"

"Animals disappearing!" Mom said. "What is the world coming to?"

chapter 5

Tuesday at school was one of the worst days possible. We had a substitute who made Felty look like the queen of Egypt. His name was Mr. Bowen, and he looked like one of those guys who thinks the world centers around PE but has to teach other subjects because there're not enough sports jobs to go around.

"Your teacher's mother is ill," he announced, "but I want you to know that there'll be no sub baiting on my shift. I believe in corporal punishment, and I'm not afraid to use it."

About ten hands went up.

"Yes," he hissed.

"What is . . . *corporal* punishment?" a boy behind me asked.

"*Corps* means the body. Like Marine Corps. A body of marines. Also, your body. Your physical being. Figure that one out, Einstein!" The hands slowly lowered. I imagined whoever had asked the question sinking pretty deep into his seat.

Mr. Bowen had a crewcut. He was a huge, muscular guy. The closest animal I can compare him to is a rhino, or a bulldog. But actually, he was more like an army tank. Most people, if you stop to think about it, move their body parts in different directions, at different times. This guy's body was so stiff and musclebound, he moved in one piece. And boy did he move. He circled and circled the classroom, looking for something for which he could nail someone: an elbow on a desk, a yawn, a sneeze that might sound faked.

I finished my language arts early. The assignment Felty had left was to write a poem about something you love. It was a dorky assignment, but I got through it easily. I wrote about the pet shop.

Having already humiliated about four students for various infractions, Mr. Bowen finally sat down at Felty's desk. Before long, he had his head buried in an issue of *Sports Illustrated* and was, like most subs, oblivious. It was then that I noticed the note being passed. It started with Karen Single, a red-haired mouse who barely ever speaks to anyone, then made its way back to Sarah James, then to Tony. When Tony got the note, he chuckled, then passed it back to me. Pretty much everyone in the class was now watching the progress of the note. Little noises erupted here and there as everyone waited for the note to get to them. I figured it was something about the Marine Corps sergeant, Mr. Athletic sub, and I unrolled it carefully, the same way I do when I have a fortune cookie message: *Sharon Trout is a stuck-up creep* is what the note said.

Sharon sits across the aisle from me. I looked over at her. She was leaning toward me, trying to get a glimpse of the message.

The kid behind me was tapping my shoulder. Tony gestured for me to pass it on.

What the note said may be true, but somehow, I couldn't pass it on. I took the note, folded it, and stuck it in my pocket. A bunch of kids, the ones who hadn't seen it, started groaning.

I wasn't paying attention to the sub, just to the kids around me. All of a sudden, there he was, right on top of me like a tank. "What did you put in your pocket?"

"Nothing." I gulped.

"Nothing, *sir*."

" 'Nothing, sir,' " I repeated. He was definitely a military type.

"Stand up."

I stood.

"Raise your arms."

I wondered what he was going to do. I once read about an American kid in Singapore who wrote graffiti on the walls and was imprisoned and beaten with a cane.

I raised my arms.

Bowen emptied out my pockets. A stick of gum, a couple of dog vitamins, a paper clip, a piece of chalk, a rubber band, and the note fell on the floor. The class laughed. Bowen bent down and picked up the note. "Let's see what you have to say about me." He unfolded the note. " 'Sharon Trout,' " he read aloud, " 'is a . . .' " He stopped. "Who is Sharon Trout?" he asked. "Is she in here?"

Sharon shyly raised her hand.

"Young man," the wicked sub said, "you will apologize to Ms. Trout."

"But I didn't write it." My voice came out kind of squeaky and scared.

"Then who did?"

I looked at Karen Single. Her eyes got wide with fear. "I don't know," I offered.

"You will stay in for recess and eat your lunch in here with me, where I will give you a very pleasant lecture on how to behave that will take your APPETITE AWAY!"

When he yelled the last couple of words, the whole class jumped, and most kids turned back to their desks. I thought of all the Roald Dahl books I'd read where kids are powerless, at the mercy of some menacing tyrant. Then I glanced over at Sharon, hoping that she knew I hadn't written it. She had her face down, buried in her arms, so I didn't know what she thought.

chapter 6

On Wednesday, Sharon Trout was absent, but Felty was back. "My mom is fine," she said. "It was a false alarm. Thank goodness." She talked on and on about hospitals and how she wanted to charge doctors for how long they made her wait. Her chatter was like music to all of us. At the end of the day, just as we were packing up, she said, "Oh, by the way, I heard that the substitute was not very nice. I'm sorry, and I've filed a request that he not be asked back to my class."

That made me feel downright cheerful. It was as if things were right in the world and justice prevailed. To celebrate, I kept Bertha company a few extra minutes on my way home, so she could tell me more nursery rhymes.

Here's a list of my chores for Wednesdays. First, I make sure that every pet is doing fine. As Sharon pointed out, it's a bummer to see a fish floating at the top of the aquarium. If anything bad has happened, I want to catch it before a customer does. Then, I move the fish from one tank to another and wash a third of the aquariums. I don't wash all of them because there are so many, so I rotate them every third week. Then I feed all the animals, restock the shelves, play with the pets who like to play, and converse with Toddy, who's supposed to be a talking bird but hasn't uttered a word.

One of the things that's traumatic about having a pet store is that pets you really like get sold.

Today, my favorite salamander, Specks, was gone. I couldn't help feeling sad. Dad says reptiles don't feel affection, but I could swear Specks came up to the glass and flashed a little grin when I came by. And when I took him out, he'd just sit on my shoulder and not try to run away.

"Who bought Specks?" I asked Dad.

He stopped to wipe some chow mein off his chin. "Specks?"

"The salamander with the yellow spots," I explained. Only Mom knows my names for them.

"No one. This has been the slowest day in the world. I could do without January all together."

"Where's Mom?"

"The vet. Twinkledoon must have a hairball the size of Texas. We tried pineapple juice, but nothing doing."

Twinkledoon is one of the Persians. We sometimes call her the Curse because customers have put deposits on her three times but never returned to get her.

"Maybe Mom sold Specks."

"Nope. There've been no sales." Dad pointed to the cash register, then returned to his chow mein. I knew not to get between him and his food. I finished my rounds and had my snack. Since Sharon wasn't in school, I figured I'd be free from her tutoring. Tony Wong had told me to come over and see his baseball cards.

"Dad, can I go out and play for a while before I finish my chores?"

"Huh?" he mumbled through a mouthful of food. "Well, it seems a bit unusual, but okay."

Wouldn't Felty be happy? She'd been lecturing me lately about breaking my rituals.

Tony was sitting on the front step of Wong's. I feel a little sorry for Tony because he lives right above his family's restaurant. I may *feel* like I live in Betts Pets, but we actually live in an apartment six blocks away. I like that.

My parents *did* live in the upstairs apartment when they were first married, and my dad's mom lived there until she died, when I was four. Now, the apartment's empty, and my mom keeps saying my dad should paint it and fix it up so we can rent it out, but he never gets around to it.

Like me, Tony spends a lot of time working in the family business, so he understands why I can't play baseball on a Saturday afternoon or join the soccer team.

Our interests are different, though. The mention of animals to him brings to mind family recipes. Plus, he has a really gross sense of humor, which is a little hard to take sometimes.

"Hey," he said when I walked up. "What's the difference between broccoli and boogers?"

"What?"

"Kids don't eat broccoli." Tony laughed his head off. He always thinks his jokes are way funnier than they are.

"Man, it's freezing." I wrapped my jacket tighter around me. I must've grown lately 'cause my wrists stuck out about four inches from my sleeves.

"It's hot in *there*." Tony pointed to his restaurant. "Know what we do to customers we don't like?"

"What?"

"Give 'em fried boogers."

"Do you wanna ruin Wong's food for me? We eat there every day!"

"Don't worry. We like you guys. We give you extra. No boogers."

"Wanna play baseball?" I decided to change the subject.

"Okay." I followed Tony upstairs so he could get his bat and mitt. He lives with his mom, dad, grandma, two sisters, and an aunt and uncle. See, his mom's Italian; his dad is Chinese. He has a whole set of Italian relatives who live in Chicago, and when they come to visit, watch out! The cooking that goes on in that house. Tony says it's a regular competition. And the food over-flows to us. It's fantastic.

The stairwell to the Wongs' apartment is really dark. It smells a lot like the food cooking downstairs, which makes the apartment seem all the more surprising when you open the door. It's beautiful. There's a big wide window looking onto the street. And every room is decorated with fancy furniture from China, paintings, statues, and vases with fresh flowers. It's immaculately clean. You would never imagine from the outside how rich it looks on the inside.

His aunt and grandma were playing backgammon. They're both supernice. "Look, there's Aaron," they said in unison. "Hi, Aaron. Long time no see."

His grandma dashed to the kitchen. She cut me a great big slab of fudge, which I popped in my mouth. Even if he does live above his shop, Tony has it pretty good; there's always someone to talk to, a table full of food (Tony says that food and love mean the same thing in his house), and lots of activity. When I go home, my dad is sitting in front of the TV, asleep, while my mom pores over the accounts. The fridge is usually empty except for a couple of gallons of milk and some crackers. There's never fudge or candy lying around on little plates.

"So, you got a girlfriend," Tony teased as we warmed up with a game of catch.

"No way!"

"Sharon Trout. Pretty classy," he joked, "for a stuck-up witch."

"She's not my girlfriend!"

"But you protected her!"

Tony tossed the ball to me. Tony's superathletic. He moves like a cheetah.

"I'll bet you could be in the major leagues when you grow up." I held up my mitt as he pitched, then was surprised to feel the ball in it. Tony picked up his bat. I pitched it back.

"That's what my dad wants me to do." He swung. The ball flew over our heads and into the alley. We've broken our share of windows together, Tony and I.

"Don't you want to?" We ran together to look for the ball.

"Nah. What do you want to be when you grow up?"

"I don't know. An artist. A zoologist."

"I'd think you'd want to get away from animals."

"I don't mind animals; I just want to work with bigger ones."

"I wanna be a chef." Tony grinned.

"No kidding?" I laughed.

"At a hotel or fancy restaurant. Funny, huh? And when someone comes in who's stuck-up, I'll spit a loogey in their food."

"Quit with that, will you? I'm gonna puke up that fudge."

"All right. All right. You've got a girl stomach, you know that?"

"It's funny that we both want to stay in the family businesses."

"Yeah, unless *you* become an artist. Speaking of art, what happens when you cross a fat face with art? A fart face! Hey, look who's here. Your girlfriend."

She was wearing her fur coat and a matching muff and hat. "Aaron Betts, we were supposed to meet at four!"

"You weren't at school, so I thought—"

"I was at the museum. Dad said I needed a mental health day from school."

"Doesn't seem like it did much good." Tony chuckled.

Sharon did look kind of teary eyed, and I felt bad, but it had been ages since I'd had time to play with Tony.

"Well, thanks for your help, Sharon, but I think I'm getting the hang of math, so I don't really need you to tutor me anymore."

"That's for Mrs. Felty to decide."

"Not today."

"But my chauffeur isn't picking me up for an hour," she whined.

Just then Tony's mom drove up. "Tony!" She climbed out of the car and grabbed a bunch of bags. "Help me haul in these groceries."

"Okay. See ya, lovebirds." He followed his mom into the restaurant.

chapter 7

"Hello, Mrs. Betts," Sharon said politely when we walked in. Mom had just taken off her coat. Twinkledoon was wrapped around her neck like a scarf.

I wanted to ask Mom about Specks but knew that if she hadn't sold him, she'd be really freaked out.

"Hello, Sharon," Mom said.

"What a pretty cat," Sharon said.

Who gave her a nice pill?

"How's *your* pet today?" Dad sauntered over. He patted the sleeve of Sharon's coat. "Well-fed, I see."

"Good afternoon, Mr. Betts," Sharon said, refusing the bait.

"I've got to do a few chores. Feed the fish and stuff," I explained. "Hope you don't mind."

"No."

I actually had to feed some insects to the reptiles, but I figured I'd do that after she left, to spare her the sight (and myself her sarcasm).

Sharon held open the top to the aquarium while I sprinkled in the food.

One of our few customers, Mr. Prescott from the car rental agency, came in. He has about twenty cats that he keeps at work with him. He comes in once a month to stock up on supplies. He's one of the people who used to live in the apartments before they burned down. "A loyal customer," Mom says.

We moved on to the next aquarium, and again Sharon helped me.

"So you got out of school today? Lucky you." I tried to strike up a conversation.

"Yeah. My mom won her finals and she has to stay in North Carolina for the whole tournament."

"Oh."

"So my dad said I could stay home." She sighed. "And . . ."

"What?"

"I really didn't want to come back if that awful substitute was there."

"Felty was back, and she promised we'd never have him again."

"Really?"

I stirred the water around in the tank and checked the filter. "Anyway, you didn't miss much. Felty brought in some masks she bought in Africa last summer. Then she went on about some dance she saw there, and she even showed us how it went."

"That's pretty scary."

"It was. She moved her arms around like this and chanted, 'Boolah, Boolah!' And the scariest thing is that one of the masks looked just like her face."

That got a smile. "Aaron. Thank you for putting that awful note in your pocket. I don't even want to know what it said."

"Hand me the food, please." I was glad she knew I didn't write it.

The door chimed. A woman wearing a long black coat and dark glasses came in. She took a quick look around the store and then walked out. I thought about the missing pets. If they were being stolen, I should consider everyone a suspect.

"You're lucky," Sharon said.

"Why?"

"You get to be with your parents all the time."

I glanced at the cash register. My dad and Mr. Prescott were leaning over Dad's crossword puzzle, arguing over who played Mammy in *Gone with the Wind*. My mom stood with Twinkledoon in front of the myna bird, trying to teach it etiquette. "Now, Toddy," she instructed in a high-pitched voice, "say hello to your friend the cat. How do you do, Twinkledoon? How do you do?" When Toddy stayed mute, she shook her finger at him. "You are a very bad boy."

"I guess," I said to Sharon.

We went to the back room. I hoped the rats, or whatever it was, wouldn't start making the strange scratching, scraping noise again. I had looked all over the room for the source of that noise, but I hadn't turned up anything, not even an escaped Ronald Reagan as I'd hoped.

"Are you really doing better in math?" Sharon asked.

"I guess."

"I am a great tutor."

Just when I was starting to like her a little, she gets like that.

I put the boxes away and organized things. She opened up my math book and smoothed the pages in a prim little gesture. "Will your mom really get that bird to talk?"

"Yeah. She's never failed. It might take her a month or two, though."

"Do the birds actually think? Or do they just imitate?"

"Well, they definitely imitate. But they also think and feel. Like this parrot we had, Mr. Scones. Whenever we sold an animal, he'd get really agitated, like he knew one of his friends was leaving for good."

"Mr. Scones?"

"My mom named him," I lied.

"Well, Toddy's pretty cool," Sharon admitted, "even if he won't do what your mom wants. But I wouldn't want to have a bird 'cause all that poop they drop on the bottom of the cage is just too gross!"

"Did you know that bird droppings are really high in calcium and magnesium and are actually a food? In fact, my dad says that maybe the manna-from-heaven stuff in the Bible was bird droppings, 'cause it's so nutritious."

"Is that what *you* eat?" she teased.

"I eat at Wong's," I offered proudly, "just about every meal."

She shrugged. "I eat at a great big table with my dad. Like in one of those old movies. It's ridiculous. If my mom's home, it's cool 'cause she's got lots of good golf stories and she's really funny. She does impersonations—"

"What's that?"

"Imitations of people. Like, 'Oh dahling, you wehr jest mahvolous on the twelfth tee.' But if it's my dad . . . well, he just sits there thinking . . . you know, like he's solving some big problem. And once in a while, he'll say something. He'll say, 'How is school?' or 'Still getting those As?' "

Sharon's eyes were round as an owl's, as if she was going to cry. I didn't know what to do.

"I'm almost done here." I closed up a couple of boxes my dad must've left open and sat down with her at the table. Within about ten minutes, we had polished off the math.

"So, what did you do your report on?" Sharon closed the book.

"Which report?"

"You know, the most fascinating person in American history."

I swallowed the glob of panic that rose into my throat. I had forgotten about my report, and I still had a ton of chores to get through.

"Oh, that. Isn't that due . . ." I was fishing for the due date.

Sharon shook her head. She looked about as smug as a snake who'd just caught a mouse. "Tomorrow!" she said. "I did mine on Eleanor Roosevelt. She redefined the role of first lady by being a woman who was a powerful force for social change."

"Sounds like you *memorized* your report."

"And *she* had this really sad childhood. Her dad died of alcoholism when she was young, and her mom died shortly after. She was amazing! So who's yours on?"

I thought quickly. "Harry Houdini."

"Houdini? What did he ever do?"

"He could escape from a vessel filled with water, wearing handcuffs!" I exclaimed. That much I knew. When I was little, I walked around for about a year doing magic tricks, saying I was a magician. "He's a regular Houdini," my dad would tell the customers.

"You haven't started yet, have you?" This time, the way she asked was kind of soft and nice.

"No," I admitted.

"You are dead meat!" She laughed.

"No kidding."

"Tell you what. I'll call Loafer and tell him to pick us up, and we can go to the library and work on your paper. They've got computers there, and everything. For five cents a page, you can print it."

"But, I've got all these chores!" I said.

"Won't your parents want you to get your schoolwork done?"

"I'll ask." We packed our books. "Loafer?" It hit me.

"That's what I call my chauffeur. Loafer the chauffeur. Aside from driving me places, all he does is sit around and wait. Pretty funny, huh?"

My mom was still in front of Toddy. "How do you do? How do you do?"

"Mom, can I go to the library?"

"Honey, you've got too many chores."

"See," I told Sharon.

"Mrs. Betts." Sharon sighed impatiently. "He has a paper that is due *tomorrow*! And he hasn't even *started* it! He has to do some research."

"Oh." Mom smiled at Sharon the way she does at kids who tap on the aquariums. "You should have said so, Aaron. Okay. Go ahead."

"But what about my chores?" I wasn't that sure I wanted to get into a car with someone named Loafer.

"They can wait. This place isn't exactly hopping, is it? We can deal with your absence." My mom sounded so tired and looked so sad that it made my stomach hurt. It was as if I'd told her I was leaving home for good rather than just going to the library for an afternoon.

Loafer was a silent type, with long hair and a big mustache. Although the day was as dark and gloomy as you could imagine, he wore sunglasses. I was surprised that anyone would hire a guy like that to cart his daughter around.

He was also the slowest driver in the world. It felt like he was going five miles an hour. As we drove past the community garden, I pointed out Bertha to Sharon. Bertha was waving her arms around, talking to an older man like she was a grand duchess giving directions to her butler.

At the library, Sharon went straight to the computers and started gathering material about Houdini. I took the old-fashioned route and sat down with a big book. There were all kinds of cool pictures of Houdini locked into one life-threatening pose or another, and pictures of him with his wife on his world travels.

I didn't know where to start, so I took out my sketchpad.

Drawing isn't just a hobby for me. A lot of times I draw when I want to understand something. Like I might feel confused or worried, and I'll take out my pad and draw as fast as I can. Whatever appears tells me something.

Houdini's body came quickly. The thing I had trouble with was the face. In photographs, his face always seemed full of confidence. It was like nobody could get one over on him. But in my drawing, every time I filled in his face, the expression was kind of sad and lost, like a little kid who's just been sent to live with foster parents, or something. It reminded me of the way Bertha looked when she finished one of her stories and saw I needed to head off.

I tried six or seven times, but I couldn't quite capture his expression. Finally, I laid down my sketchpad and started reading the book.

Houdini was the son of a rabbi. I was interested in that. My mom's from a Jewish family. My dad's family was Methodist. But neither of my parents is particularly religious. In fact, I'd say that animals are their religion.

Houdini grew up very poor, developing his skills slowly, making a meager living performing his feats until success finally came.

He was very attached to his mom, the book said, and when she died, he was "inconsolable."

Houdini died of appendicitis after an overly exuberant fan punched him in the stomach before he had time to tense his muscles to protect himself.

I looked back at my sketch of him and then figured something out. Houdini was the master of illusion, of appearances. I think the way I drew him was the way he kinda felt inside: scared and alone. I had the slant for my paper. Mrs. Felty is big on having a slant. She says you can't just write the facts; you have to have something else to layer over them, like a theme. I'd write about the differences between his outside self and inside self.

That's the way it is with most people, I think. There's the way they appear, and there's the way they really are, deep inside.

chapter 8

🐜 "How's the tutoring going?" Mrs. Felty asked me the next day.

"I still don't really get it," I admitted.

"Well, it must be osmosis, because you got an A on your quiz."

I wasn't sure what *osmosis* meant, but I was pretty happy about that. It was probably the first time I'd gotten an A on anything in math since second grade. I would've skipped home if I didn't need to count the steps.

Like I said, I'm not a person who likes change. So you can imagine how surprised I was when I stopped at the lot and saw that the dinosaur skeleton had been torn down. There were people all over the place: men and women in suits and hardhats, with cell phones. Bulldozers were plowing up the earth like there was no tomorrow. I almost lost count of my steps!

The guys with the brown paper bags and the people with shopping carts full of cans were gone. Only Bertha was left, perched on her folding chair at the edge of the garden, hugging herself against the icy wind.

In front of her was a man in a bright yellow hardhat, yelling at her like she was deaf. "For the last time! Will you get up and move along?"

Bertha tugged her ski cap farther down on her forehead. She peered up at the man: "Cinderella met a fella, dancing down the hall. Said Cinderella to the fella, 'Come with me to the ball.' Said the fella to Cinderella, 'Why don't we just dance here?' Said Cinderella to the fella, 'So good to feel you near!' My name is Bertha."

"I don't care what your name is. My instructions are to level this lot." He touched her elbow. Bertha yanked away with what looked like a lot of strength. She clutched the arms of her chair.

"I'm not speaking to you," she said. "You're a bad man."

"Listen! It ain't public property anymore, and you'll have to leave . . . unless you'd like to spend a few days in jail!"

"Three blind mice." She put her hands over her ears. "Three blind mice. See how they play Parcheesi and talk in tongues. No way, Jose. This is *my* garden. My name is Bertha."

This time, he pulled her very roughly by the arms.

"Get your hands off of her!" I ran over.

Startled for a second, he let go. "Or you'll . . . what?" He took off his hardhat.

"Or I'll . . . sue you!" I couldn't think of anything else. The guy weighed about three hundred pounds.

"What"—he snickered—"you her lawyer?"

"You can't ruin the garden. There're people who live off of this food."

"Looks like a bunch of dead weeds to me."

"There're probably some potatoes or something . . . some cabbage—"

"Who cares?" he interrupted.

"And in the spring, there's even more. There're all kinds of vegetables and flowers! This garden belongs to a *bunch* of people!"

"Not anymore, kid." The man sighed. It was as if his anger deflated like a balloon. "You want a beam to fall on her head? You want her to get mowed down by a steamroller? This is private property, purchased and owned by L. Q. Cross and Company. This here will be Cross Downs, luxury condominiums."

"I thought it was going to be a housing project."

"Haven't you heard of urban renewal, kid? Mr. Cross purchased this property from the city."

What he was saying would be good for Betts Pets and Wong's, but I'd had something different in mind. I'd pictured the garden getting bigger and bigger, then the dinosaur being finished and the gardeners moving right into it.

"Just go home, lady!" he said.

"My name is Bertha," she repeated.

"What if she doesn't have a home?" I offered.

At that, he shifted and looked back at her and then at me. "That's not my problem," he finally said.

"It seems it *is*!" I lost my temper, and for a minute, I knew what it felt like to be Sharon Trout and just say any old thing you felt like, no matter how obnoxious.

"I can put you in jail, too, you know. They have jails for kids," he said.

Bertha stuck out her tongue at him.

"Kids," he mumbled. "Misguided kids. Fine! Let her sit there and be injured—and all for a few potatoes!" Then he walked away.

"I think you'll have to find someplace else, Bertha." I tried to explain. "There must be other places where you can garden."

"Geese fly south for the winter, Captain," she said, hugging her arms around herself to block the wind.

I wished she could do the same.

chapter 9

When I got to the shop, Dad was on his usual perch by the cash register. He was working on his crossword puzzle, completely absorbed.

"Dad!" I tugged his sleeve. He didn't respond. "Dad!"

"What's four letters, 'one who is a man-eating giant or monster,' starts with *o*?"

"I don't know," I said. But I know how stubborn my dad is; he can't move on from a thought unless he's thoroughly satisfied. I tried thinking about all the man-eating giants and monsters I could, but all I kept seeing was the guy in the hardhat.

"There's the beanstalk giant," Dad mused.

"*Ogre!*" The word popped into my head. My thoughts are like that. They never come when I'm looking for them, but always later.

"Bingo!" He wrote it in.

"Dad!"

"Huh?"

"We've got to do something. They're building a condominium complex on the city lot, and this guy is pushing Bertha around."

"Who?"

"They're going to ruin the garden!"

"A condominium complex?" he said slowly. "You mean the housing project?"

"It's not going to be a housing project," I explained as patiently as I could. "It was bought by some rich guy, and now it's going to be something Downs, luxury condominiums."

"Hmmm. That should be good for business."

"I know. But right now, we need to do something about Bertha!"

"Who's Bertha?"

"My friend!"

"The nursery-rhyme lady?"

"Come on!" I tugged his sleeve. He stood up. I could tell he didn't really understand what I was saying, but he was willing to come along for the ride. If there's one thing that interests my dad, it's buildings going up and buildings coming down. We were almost to the door when he stopped suddenly. "Wow," he said, "that was a close call."

"What?"

"Your mom. She's at the grocery store. There's no one to mind the shop."

"Great." I sighed. "By the time we get there, she'll probably have been flattened by a bulldozer."

"I don't think they'll just plow your friend under, Aaron. That's not rational. Your mom will be back any second. Then we'll go. Nine letters. Means 'artificial.' Starts with an *s*; ends with *c*."

"*Synthetic*," I offered, surprising myself.

"I guess you *are* learning something in school." He wrote in the word.

Just then, my mom walked in with a few bags. "I thought I'd make some sandwiches for a change," she said.

I dragged my dad toward the door. "Be right back!" I shouted.

"Some adventure or another, Muriel," Dad explained, following me.

It was almost dark. The wind had died down. The clouds lowered in on us, like we were under some great big bird that was closing up its wings.

I ran to Bertha's spot. She was gone. I looked around for the man in the hardhat, but all I saw were two men in suits. One was talking on his cell phone; the other was poring over some plans. I was about to give up, when I spotted the black-and-white police car. Between the front and back seats was a cagelike divider to keep criminals from getting to the cops. Sitting in that back seat was Bertha. Her ski cap was pulled down low over her eyes. As the cop got into the driver's seat, Bertha turned and looked over at me. I called to my dad, then ran toward the police car. Bertha smiled sadly and waved at me as the car pulled away.

I don't know how many police departments there are in Cleveland, but I'll bet there's about a hundred. Every area has a precinct. Some precincts even have two or three stations. Dad explained this to me as we walked to the car. He still didn't seem to understand what was happening, but he was willing to go along. It's one of the things I like about my dad. He doesn't come up with things to do on his own that often, but if I come up with something, like tickets to a ball game or an idea about going down to the riverfront and throwing stones, he's usually game. My mom's the same. Easygoing.

Our local station hadn't arrested anyone, and just our luck, the desk captain knew my dad, had bought a cocker spaniel from us about six years ago. The guy couldn't stop talking about him. "So's I take Burger out with me hunting, and he, man-oh-man, is he the best hunting dog in this city or country. I trained him to answer to this whistle. It's a high-pitched thing that only dogs can hear . . ." He went on and on, and, of course, my dad was fascinated. You'd think he'd get tired of hearing about housetraining and dog commands, but he never does. It's like every story is being told for the first time. When the officer ran to his office to get pictures of Burger, I whispered to my dad, "A two-word command that means 'to depart.' "

He looked perplexed. Then he said. "Okay, buddy."

Dad looked at the pictures quickly, wowed over the cocker's "feathers," the long ruffled fur around their ears and belly, then asked his friend where Bertha might be taken. The cop launched into a long lecture about "vagrants" and the damage they do. Finally, he made a call, then said that there'd been a pickup two stations over.

Dad tried to talk me into forgetting about everything and heading to Cuzzie's for hot fudge sundaes. A hot fudge sundae sounded great, but I insisted we look for Bertha.

This time, the cop at the desk wasn't nearly as friendly. He was a short, skinny guy with little ferret eyes that blinked at us like we were predators or something.

"We're looking for Bertha." I decided to take control of the situation.

"Who?"

"The woman who was picked up at Chestnut and Thirty-third," Dad explained.

"Everyone's looking for someone," he said snidely.

"Is she here?" Dad asked.

"You family?"

"No."

"Friends?"

Dad looked at me.

"Not exactly," I said.

"I ain't giving you any information," he said.

"Can we visit her?"

"What's her last name?" the cop said.

"I don't know," Dad said.

"You don't *know*?"

Just then a woman cop came to the desk. She was very pretty, like a cop on TV. She had dark skin, long shiny panther hair down her back, in a braid, and beautiful white teeth. I wondered what she was doing in a police station when she should be modeling toothpaste, smiling down on the city from a billboard. "What's up, Brady?"

"These folks are looking for someone who's been brought in."

"Bertha!" I said. I knew if there was one thing Bertha would've told them, it was her name.

"Oh." She smiled. "Lovely lady. She's just been released."

"Where?"

"I'm sorry," she said, "but I don't know. I mean, we don't really throw people into the slammer just for a bit of loitering." She winked at me. I knew she was trying to be nice, but it somehow made me feel worse, like everything was a big game without human stakes. "She assured us she'd go straight home."

"Then she had someplace to go?" I asked.

"She definitely had an address," the lady said.

"Can you —" I started to ask for her address, thinking that maybe Dad and I could drop in, bring her a hamburger or something, and help her find another place to plant her vegetables.

"I'm sorry," the lady cop interrupted. "I can't give that information out."

"See, Aaron? She's been released. Now let's go get some hot fudge sundaes."

"Watch those calories," the lady cop said, eyeing Dad's girth.

"I will." Dad smiled. "Starting tomorrow!"

"Good plan." She threw a dirty look at Brady before she walked away.

"Feel better?" Dad said.

I really didn't, although I did appreciate the lady cop. It's funny. It only takes a little niceness to make a big difference.

"A banana split sounds okay," I admitted.

chapter 10

For the next couple of weeks, I looked for Bertha. In the lot, a building began to form. Where in the summer there had been sunflowers, nasturtiums, tomatoes, lettuce, and peas was now a slab of concrete for a parking lot.

It seemed to happen overnight.

Of course, my dad had a commentary on that: "It took a hundred years to build the Coliseum, but they're putting up this one in thirty days. I wouldn't house a paper doll there!"

"Now, Pop," Mom said, "remember your blood pressure."

"My blood pressure's so low, I could be dead."

He'd been cranky since that day we looked for Bertha. Over banana splits, I'd laid out the whole story to him about Bertha and how it worried me that now she wouldn't have anywhere to grow vegetables or hang out during the day, or even worse, there would be no one to listen to her speeches.

"I'm sure she could find a nice park or something," he offered. Then he went on one of his tirades about how the tax money had all been spent on legal battles and scandals instead of useful things.

"She definitely seems like a nut, so I hope she's not in a nut house," Sharon commented when I told her about Bertha.

"Mental institution," Mom corrected. Mom was shuffling around the storeroom, looking for some birdseed that had disappeared.

"'Cause in nut houses," Sharon explained, "they let the inmates sleep in their own poop and don't feed them, and they keep the violent ones with everyone else—"

"They're *patients*, Sharon," Mom argued, "and I don't think conditions are like that anymore. They were once . . ."

🐜 🐜 🐜

After Mom left, Sharon closed the math book. I'd actually been getting somewhere with all the studying. Maybe it was osmosis, like Felty said. I'd looked up the word, and it means "the gradual assimilation of facts, ideas, or habits that seems to occur without conscious or deliberate effort." (It also means "the diffusion of a fluid through a semipermeable membrane, resulting in equalization of the pressures on each side," but I'm sure Felty meant the first one.)

My grades had improved, and Felty said I didn't need tutoring until the next "transition," meaning until we moved on to some new stuff, but Sharon and I were still polishing up my skills, doing drills, just being sure I got it. More and more, I must admit, our conversation drifted to other subjects.

"It's a mystery," Sharon said. "And I love a mystery."

"What's a mystery?"

"The disappearance of Bertha."

"I'll tell you another mystery," I said.

"What?"

"Two more pets have disappeared. A gerbil and a frog."

"Did you tell your mom?"

"No. I didn't want to upset her."

"I'm surprised she didn't notice."

"Well, I take care of the gerbils, and they're always hiding in their litter or their playground. And the frogs camouflage themselves. Besides, she's been really distracted. And something else . . ."

"What?"

"Supplies are missing, too. She thinks she forgot to order the birdseed. Well, I did the inventory last week, and we're missing more than birdseed."

"Wow. Maybe your mom and dad should install video cameras."

"Yeah. This kid came in last Saturday with his mom, and he wanted a snake really bad. His mom was after a puppy, and she told him that she didn't like reptiles and stuff. He knocked over the rack that has all the pet care books, ran around like a little maniac, screaming and crying."

"Weird!"

"But I figure that someone must've stolen stuff during all the commotion. Otherwise, I don't know."

"We've got to figure this out. Two mysteries. *I* know!"

"What?"

"Houdini!"

"Huh?"

"Magic! You know how you said Houdini could get in and out of places with a combination of 'will and skill.' "

"Yeah."

"Well, there's a clue in that. Who can get in and out of the cages?"

"You might as well say there's a clue in Eleanor Roosevelt."

"Don't be silly. But wait! Maybe there is to the mystery of Bertha, because Eleanor Roosevelt was one of the first first ladies to really deal with social issues. When there were these starving coal miners and stuff, she helped them build a town that would really function as a community. And when the Daughters of the American Revolution wouldn't let Marian Anderson sing a concert in the Constitution Hall because she was black, Mrs. Roosevelt quit the DAR and invited her to sing on the steps of the Lincoln Memorial."

Sharon's face was all lit up. If she'd told me she was going to run for president that very moment, I'd have believed her.

chapter 11

Once in a while, on a weekend, my mom gets inspired. Then, instead of cereal or Pop-Tarts, she makes a full-on breakfast. The smell of coffee, eggs, tofu bacon (almost as good as the real stuff), and pancakes wakes me up.

One of my favorite things to do on the weekend is to remember my dreams. I always stay in bed for a few minutes, relive the good parts, analyze the bad. Then I write them down in a notebook. If it's possible, I also draw them. They end up pretty weird when I do, like pictures by that artist Dali, who used to paint his dreams of melting clocks and stuff.

In last night's dream, I was running through this maze, being chased by Sharon Trout.

In third grade, for a science project, I built a maze like the one in my dream. I took a big box and cut up some cardboard and pieced it together, with a wedge of cheese at the end. I borrowed the mice from our shop, and Dad came along to make sure they were treated right. When it came time to put a mouse in, I picked our fastest mouse, Harvey. Harvey was Ronald Reagan's great-granddad. Harvey took one look at that maze and went on strike. He curled up in the entrance corner and fell asleep.

In my dream, the maze was made out of white poster board. On the walls were fractions of all shapes and sizes. I got to the end, expecting my piece of cheese, but instead, there were three white mice sitting in little foldup chairs, like the kind directors use. And they were wearing dark glasses. It took me a minute to figure out why. They were blind.

By the time I got dressed and made my way to the kitchen, Mom and Dad were eating away. They both eat like they're always in a hurry. They could be members of Congress, the way they act, like they've got something pressing on them, like it's the Joint Security Council rather than just a few dirty cages to clean.

"Something has to be done," I heard my mom whisper. "We're a month behind on our rent here. The landlord just sent a nasty letter. You can't get water from a rock."

"We've always had the shop. It's our life," Dad said.

"Well, maybe we could change locations."

"That takes capital," my dad said. "And money is what we don't have."

"We have to sell the shop." My mom said it firmly. I could hear the choked sound in her voice, the way she sounds when she's gonna cry but doesn't want to do it in front of us.

"No one is going to buy that shop. What are we going to show them for earnings? For potential?"

"We'll just have to sell the building, then, and find jobs," Mom said. "I can get a teaching job—"

I was about to go in, but I waited. I knew it was wrong to listen in, but I had about as much chance of learning the truth otherwise as I did of becoming a master of calculus. I held my breath and tried to be perfectly still.

"How much could we possibly get for the building?" my dad interrupted. "The neighborhood's gone downhill so much, it's worthless."

"Well, what do you suggest?"

"I don't know. I just know that I can't let go of Betts Pets. It's been my family's life for generations, and it's our life."

My mom sighed. "I know. I know. But right now, all those animals are costing us more than we're making."

"It's the conglomerations!" My dad banged his fist on the table. He hardly ever gets mad about anything, but when he does, it's usually about the conglomerations. "Big business is swallowing the little man! Swallowing him whole!"

"Shhh," Mom said. "Aaron will hear."

At that point, I made a little noise, like footsteps, and walked into the kitchen.

"Hot breakfast," Mom said cheerfully. "We've got to vamoose in forty minutes."

Saturday's the one day of the week when we still get some business. That's when all the looky-loos come in just to stare at the pets, like we're a zoo or something, and also when people decide to buy their dog food, kitty litter, or whatever.

Most kids play on Saturdays, but I work the cash register. And my dad's right. I do a good job. Even though I've done it for years, I still think it's cool to punch in the numbers on our old register, hear the loud ring, and watch the drawer fling open. I like to answer questions about how to care for birds, train puppies, and keep cats from scratching up the furniture. On Saturdays, our place still feels like a real shop.

But today was different. Today, I looked around at everything like I was seeing it for the last time. I tried to picture the rooms empty and the windows boarded up like on so many other storefronts around us. I know I like to complain, but I couldn't imagine life without the birds chirping, the mice squeaking, the door chiming, the aquariums gurgling. I looked over at my dad. He was explaining to a man how to balance an aquatic habitat, the need for bottom feeders and plants. My dad spent about half an hour answering the man's questions. Then the man walked out without buying a thing.

chapter 12

The next day arrived all dressed up to match my mood. The sky was gray and ice cold. A heavy drizzle flowed down the pane of my window, as if an oversize snowman were on the roof crying big tears.

I didn't want to get out of bed.

Didn't want to venture into the kitchen and listen in on another depressing conversation.

The phone rang. I heard my mom answer. I imagined it was our landlord calling to remind her that we were a month behind on our rent. To tell the truth, the guy shouldn't even charge rent for this place. The tiles in the shower are so old that whatever's growing on them won't come off, no matter how many times Mom sprays with "scrubbing bubbles." The toilet runs. The carpet curls up in places, tripping my dad on a daily basis, and it's so worn-out, you can see the gold padding underneath.

Still, it's the only home I've known. There are two bedrooms, the kitchen, and the living room, where we eat most of our meals in front of the TV, watching the pet or the history channel. Our life isn't fancy like Sharon's, but it's fun, predictable.

A month behind! If this were one of those old-fashioned English novels, we'd already have been kicked out into the snow. We'd be pressing our faces against the window of Wong's, our tongues hanging out, begging for food.

I heard Mom chatting on the phone. Her voice was relaxed, so I knew it wasn't the landlord. It made me feel better somehow. I grabbed my sketchpad.

I'd been dreaming about these strange creatures. They were a combination of animal and person. They had big bear bodies but with hands and feet and human faces.

I started to draw the figures from my dream in great detail: the individual strands of hair, the maplike lines inside their thumbs and fingers — lifelines, love lines, journey lines. That's the magic of drawing. It's just lines and more lines. Then, abracadabra; something out of nothing!

One of my favorite writers when I was little was Maurice Sendak. I remember hearing him say in an interview that the characters in his books were really his relatives in disguise.

Looking at my sketch, I had to admit that the big fat bear-man looked a whole lot like my dad. I wondered what Felty's *Psychology Today* would say about that? One minute Houdini's expression becomes Bertha's, now this.

"Aaron!" my mom called. I didn't answer. Mom mumbled something into the phone and hung up. It didn't occur to me that the phone might be for me.

I shut my sketchbook, remembering the homework I had for the weekend, sniffing for a good breakfast like yesterday's but not smelling anything.

Mom and Dad were still in their pajamas. Sundays are the easy day because we're only open from one to four. Dad was dozing in his easy chair, with the comics on his lap. Mom was cleaning the oven. "Hey, dear. Your little friend called."

"Tony?"

"Sharon."

"Is that who you were talking to?"

"Yes. She's a nice girl, actually, once you get past her attitude."

"What did she want?"

"She said to remind you that you have math home-work and that she'll be over soon to help you."

"Over where?" I groaned. It's true, I liked her a little better, but I wasn't quite sure I wanted to spend every waking minute with Sharon Trout.

"Here. I invited her here."

"Here?" I looked around. Our furniture was inherited from my dad's parents, and it looked it. The only decorations in the room were some planets I'd hung from the TV antennae when I was in first grade, after an astronomy project. Saturn had lost its rings, and Mars had peeled down to its original Styrofoam. Hung with the round planets, the TV looked like an insect with tentacles and many eyes. On the wall where there used to be a painting, a big white square, an inverse shadow, showed how filthy the walls had become.

"Isn't it kind of . . . messy?" I whispered, as tactfully as I could.

My mom shrugged. "At least the oven's clean."

I went to my bedroom and picked up my socks, baseball mitt, old shoes, and books from the floor. I had to admit my room was the nicest in the house. The window looked out on the street where a row of elms stood with their arms stretched way out into the air. Mom had framed some of my favorite drawings and hung them around the room. My bedspread was new, and I had two baseball glove chairs that were pretty cool, although I doubted a girl like Sharon would appreciate that.

I got dressed quickly.

"Hi, Mrs. Betts." I heard Sharon's voice.

"Don't mind Mr. Betts," Mom whispered about Dad, who was snoring away on the couch. "This morning's activities of drinking coffee and reading the paper have tired him out."

"Is Aaron up yet?"

"Yes, he just woke up. Would you like a Pop-Tart?"

"Sure. I don't get to eat junk food at home. Do you have any Coke?"

"No. I'm afraid Pop-Tarts are as junky as we get."

I made my appearance. Sharon was sitting at the table, munching on the Pop-Tart, swinging her legs like a little kid. "Did you forget about math?" she scolded.

"How could I? Maybe we should go to the library and do it."

"Library's closed," Sharon said. "It's Sunday. Remember?"

"Don't you go to church?" I asked, hopeful.

"Not when my mom's away. Don't you?"

"No."

My mom finished up the oven and stood back. "I do love a clean oven."

To my surprise, Sharon didn't comment on the seediness of our apartment. For lack of a better place, we went into my room. I'd never had a girl in my room before, and it was pretty weird. "Do I sit in this?" Sharon pointed to my baseball glove chair. She sat down before I could answer. "It reminds me of King Kong holding Fay Wray in his big hand. Remember that?"

"I guess."

"It's kinda romantic, don't you think? The way the gorilla loves her."

"I guess." *Why do girls have to say stuff like that?*

We whizzed through the homework. Math is like one of my rituals, I realized; you work out a certain system and memorize it. No matter what curve you're thrown, you apply the system. I was definitely catching on.

It was eleven o'clock when we finished. By that point, my mood was a little better and I didn't mind if she hung around.

"What do you want to do now?" I asked.

"Well," she said slowly, "I was hoping we could go to your store and look at the animals and stuff."

So that was it. I felt relieved. She didn't want me to be her boyfriend or anything; she just liked hanging out with our pets as much as I did.

"Sure," I said. "We'll go now. It's cool being there before we open the doors — just playing around and stuff. And I've got to clean the hamster cages."

"Cool. Will your mom mind?"

"No," I bragged. "It's my shop as much as theirs, you know? It's been passed down, generation to generation."

After I said that, I felt stupid, because it wasn't going to happen. My generation would be where it stopped, because everyone wanted to shop in big malls and shopping centers, and no one cared about the little guy. My dad had said it enough, and I knew it was true.

"What's wrong?" Sharon asked.

"Nothing."

We walked along in silence. We had to walk really close to the buildings to avoid being dripped on by the melting snow. It's about six blocks, and we walked slowly in the quiet Sunday air. I usually count my steps from this direction, too, but I made a point of not doing it.

"Do you ever feel like an actor?" Sharon broke the silence.

"Huh?"

"Like an actor in your own life?"

"What do you mean?"

"Well, my dad expects certain things from me, so I act the way he wants me to. And my mom thinks I should be real cheerful about the fact that she's always winning tournaments and stuff, but I'm just mad at her for never being home."

"Doesn't she ever take you?"

"Yeah. Summers, she does. And it's fun. My mom has a great personality."

I nodded. Was this the ways girls always talked? *Did I ever feel like an actor!* Weird question.

"Let's go past the condo complex. I want to see how far they've gotten," I said.

"Okay."

The building was coming along. You could actually see the little compartments that would be bedrooms, kitchens, bathrooms, the places where people would sit by themselves and wonder how to meet other people, the places where people would laugh and eat, where kids would play. I once saw pictures of a building in North Carolina that had been cut in half by a hurricane. It was strange. You could see the furniture, and paintings on the walls, everything intact the way it was before the place was split in two. Like looking into a dollhouse. I wished they would leave the front off this building; then you could just watch people's lives. That's what it's like with the animals in their cages or their aquariums. That's what fascinates people.

"How long has this fence been up?" Sharon asked.

"'Bout a week. Ugly, isn't it?"

"Really ugly."

"Reminds me of a prison." The fence was chainlink with barbed wire coiled around the top. I climbed as far up the fence as I could. "I guess it's good that they're building condominiums, but I miss the garden. In the summer, you should've seen it. All kinds of people came here with their gardening tools and baskets. There was this one lady who sang the whole time she worked. She had an awesome voice. Then there was a guy in a wheelchair who brought a big container of lemonade and passed out drinks. And Bertha would be talking nonstop, of course. When we had puppies, I'd bring 'em down here and let 'em run around. Everyone got a kick out of that, even the guys standing around drinking would come and play with them."

"You know what, Aaron Betts?" Sharon whispered. "I'm glad Mrs. Felty asked me to tutor you in math."

I thought about Tony teasing me about Sharon being my girlfriend. Then I thought about how sad it would be when all the pets were sold and Mom taught all day. I could picture my dad sitting in front of the TV, circling the want ads, then getting some awful job with a mean boss. My dad had never had a boss in his life. And I'd try to be cheerful and take care of the house, try to act like everything was okay. We all would. Did I ever feel like I was an actor? Yes, I guess I did.

chapter 13

As soon as I opened the door and the pets heard my voice, they started moving around and squawking in whatever language they spoke. "I just have a couple of cages to clean," I said. "Then we can just mess around."

"I'll help!" She took off her coat. "Notice I didn't wear my fur coat today?"

"Oh yeah." I hadn't.

"Fur coats are gross. Your dad's right. Who wants to wear a dead animal."

"Right." I pulled out the hamsters and loaded them into a bucket, then hauled the cages to the big sink.

"I only wear it 'cause my dad bought it for me and he expected me to be real thrilled."

"Well, it must be kind of nice, being rich and all. This cage weighs a ton."

"What can I do?" Sharon rolled up her sleeves.

"Run some hot water and put soap in." I pulled out the bottom of the cage. I expected her to comment about the hamster droppings as I swept them into the trash, but she didn't say anything. She took the emptied tray from me and put it in the sink. She scrubbed at the bottom like she'd been doing it her whole life.

"Pretty good," I admitted.

"Thanks."

While Sharon cleaned cages, I checked to see if any more animals were missing; none were.

When I came back, she was adding food and water.

"Good job," I told her.

"Mrs. Felty's getting married," Sharon said.

"You're kidding." I was genuinely surprised. I'd always imagined that Felty was about a hundred years old. Who married ladies that old?

"Nope."

"How do you know?"

"I was in the principal's office, taking a call from my dad, and I overheard the secretary talking about Mrs. Felty's wedding shower."

"Who'd want to marry Felty?"

"My mom says there's someone for everyone," Sharon said. "Okay, this one's finished."

"I hope she goes on a long honeymoon."

"Remember Christmas break, when she took a trip to Spain and brought back those maracas and the flamenco video?"

"Oh yeah."

"I guess that's where she met her husband."

"So why do we always call her *Mrs.* Felty if she hasn't been married?"

"I guess she has, a long time ago. Her first husband died."

"Boy, you sure know a lot about everyone."

"Are you going to get married someday, Aaron?"

"Come see this old cash register."

When I pushed the buttons and the drawer flew open, Sharon jumped.

"Wow! That thing is loud."

"When my mom wanted to trade it in for a computerized model, I wouldn't let her," I said.

Sharon ran her hand along the keys. "Isn't it romantic that your parents get to work together all the time?"

"I guess. As long as it lasts," I said without thinking.

"What do you mean? Are they having marriage problems?"

"No. Not that. It's just . . . business isn't so hot. My mom says we may have to move upstairs to cut costs."

"Upstairs? Oh yeah, you said there's an apartment. Well, that wouldn't be too bad."

"My mom refers to her days living there as 'the dark ages,' so I don't think it's too good."

"Well, let's go up and see for ourselves."

The idea made sense. I hadn't been there since first grade, after my mom's parents died in an accident, and we unloaded boxes of their stuff into the main room. I remember it as very small with some kind of bright red velvety wallpaper that someone must've thought was fashionable a few centuries ago.

"I don't have a key."

"What about that key ring in the cash register? Isn't there a key on there?"

"Maybe." Suddenly I was really sorry I'd let my guard down and confessed to Sharon Trout. I could imagine her telling everyone in school: Aaron is poor and has to live in a little, dark, red-velvet hovel. "It's probably really filthy and musty up there. I mean . . . if you have allergies or something."

"I don't have allergies!" She grabbed the key ring. "Besides, it's an adventure."

We walked up the stairwell. It smelled like an entrance to a bar, like stale beer, dust, and other unpleasant things (if you get my point). I expected Sharon to hold her nose and go, "Ewwww." Instead, she gave me a shove. "Go on!"

I walked to the first landing and then started up the second set of stairs. Halfway up, Sharon grabbed my pant leg. "Listen," she hissed.

I stopped and waited. Then, I heard it. The low scratching sound. It was part of what I heard from the storeroom. What was missing was the voice—the low singing voice that sounded like it was floating in the air. "Someone's in there," Sharon said.

"Let's go back," I whispered.

"Maybe it's Bertha!" she said, and that seemed so far-fetched and strange that I laughed aloud.

"You've read too many Nancy Drew books," I said, but I must admit that I thought about Bertha singing "Three Blind Mice" to me the day after the mouse had disappeared.

"Aaron, go on. We'll just open the door a little and peek in." She pushed me again.

"Okay! Okay! Keep your pants on."

"I'm wearing a dress!"

"Well, why are you wearing a dress in this weather?"

"You're stalling."

I walked up the remaining stairs and fumbled with the keys. I tried enough keys that if there was someone in there, they definitely would have heard me. "I can't find the right key."

Sharon put her hand on the doorknob, turned it, and the door swung open. It wasn't even locked.

It was there, all right, the bright velvety wallpaper, although it had faded in places into a dull pink. If I had to live day in, day out with that wallpaper, I'd lose my appetite; that was for sure.

We stepped into the dark room. Sharon crossed to a window and flung open the heavy curtains.

I'm not sure which of us gasped first.

There, in front of us on a long, wide table, was a miniature pet store.

Specks was situated in an old aquarium. It wasn't one of ours, and it had a long crack on the side of it, but other than that, it was well appointed. Part of a window screen had been cut and taped over the top so he couldn't escape. And hiding behind an assortment of plants and rocks was Bermuda, the frog.

Ronald Reagan was in a strangely constructed cage made of what looked like melted plastic. There were tunnels, air holes, and a wheel rigged up out of a milk carton.

Elvis Presley, the hamster, was in a similar environment.

The two goldfish were in a huge jar that looked like an upside-down light fixture. There was a plastic plant and a little toy wheel to keep them company.

Next was an amazing birdcage made out of copper-colored wire. It was molded in a circular design with elaborate curling lines on the side, like clef notes. The missing birdseed was beside the cage. And inside were two parakeets. I hadn't missed them because Mom had brought the new batch in while I was at school.

I checked each and every animal. They all had food and water and clean cages. They looked fine.

"Wow!" Sharon said. "Your missing pets are in your own apartment."

"I don't get it."

"Let's look for clues."

We walked around the apartment, looking in cupboards, behind boxes, under old furniture covered in dust.

There was nothing. Nothing to give a sign of who'd been here taking care of the animals.

"Hey, I found something," Sharon said. "Does this belong to you?" She held out an old felt cap. It was navy blue, and on the front was an embroidered gold anchor.

"I don't think so," I said, although the cap looked vaguely familiar.

"This is definitely a mystery," Sharon said. "And you know what comes next?"

I was afraid to ask. "What?"

"A stakeout."

"You mean we just wait here?"

"All day and all night."

"We can't stay here all night."

"Yes, we can. We'll pretend we're having a sleepover."

"On a school night?"

Sharon sighed and rolled her eyes. "Tomorrow is a teachers' workday. Remember? So it's not a school night."

I thought for a minute. I'd never slept away from home, unless it was with my parents, but it was clear that there was no way I was going to get out of this. "I've never lied to my parents," I said.

"Let me tell you something, Aaron," Eleanor Roosevelt Jr. said. "Ethics are not just about truth and untruth. We are doing something important here. And you can lie in such a way as you're not. You can say, 'Sharon and I are having a sleepover.' Unless, that is, you're afraid."

That settled it. "Okay. I'll do it, but on only one condition . . ."

"What?"

"Tony comes, too."

"Over my dead body." She stuck her finger into Ronald Reagan's cage. He sniffed at it, then licked her like he was a dog.

chapter 14

"What's in that container?" I asked.

Tony popped open one of the white to-go boxes. A delicious odor floated into the room. He had about ten boxes from his restaurant all lined up on a tray. "Lettuce-wrapped bean curd with cilantro and ginger," Tony said.

"Smells fantastic."

Tony pulled out a lo mein noodle and bit into it. "Did you know if you cut a worm in half, both sides of it will still move? It's like you've created twins."

I ignored him. "I'm gonna have a little of everything."

"Where's Sharon?" He shoveled the lo mein onto a paper plate.

"I don't know. She said she'd be here."

"She won't be here. She'll be too chicken. *Pluck. Pluck. Pluck. Pluck.*"

"Hey, quiet. Someone'll hear. Remember the point of this? To catch whoever's prowling around stealing pets."

"It's creepy up here." Tony peered at the dusty curtains. The single light bulb from the kitchen cast strange shadows on the living-room walls.

"Yeah." I perused my soon-to-be home. "Maybe we should just go to your house and sleep. We can watch out the window—"

"Now, don't get scared on me."

"I'm not scared," I argued. "It's just that . . ."

"What?"

"What if the guy who's been hiding out up here has a gun or something?"

"Then I'll jump on his neck. And you kick the gun, straight up in the air, like you see in the movies."

"Right!" I could just picture us, running around like two cartoon characters, our legs spinning like wheels.

"Listen," I whispered.

"That's just the sun setting."

"You can't *hear* the sun set." I laughed. *What a joker.*

"Oh yes, you can. Ask my grandma. There's a moment, before it slides below the horizon, when it hisses like the smallest snake on the planet. *Hisssss*."

"Shhh."

There *were* sounds, lots of them: the curtains brushing against the wallpaper, the breeze whistling through thin cracks in the window, the creaking of the walls. They were regular sounds, nothing to write home about, but enough to give me a huge case of the creeps.

If I were home, I'd be perusing my *National Geographic* before taking my bath and going to bed. My mom would bring me a glass of milk. And I wouldn't have lied to her.

Sharon and I had waited for Betts Pets to close; then we had returned the animals to their cages downstairs. After that, we waited for the culprit. We watched out the window, *spied*, until the boredom of it made me feel like I would confess to the crime myself, like a torture victim.

"If I have to keep quiet all night, we might as well go to my place," Tony said.

"No, we better stay here and be sure Sharon isn't going to show up. It would be pretty bad for her to come here by herself."

"She won't come."

"I think she will, if she can get out."

"Bet she doesn't."

"Bet she does."

"How much?"

"Dollar?"

"Okay."

We shook.

"Do you even *have* a dollar?" Tony asked.

"I've got about six hundred dollars," I said, "in a savings account." I startled myself. To be honest, I never much think about it. Every month, my parents pay me a little for working in the shop, and I deposit it in the savings account. I suddenly felt cheered. Six hundred dollars had to be enough for at least one month's rent.

I dug into the food. It was delicious. In addition to the Chinese food, Tony's dad had added some Vietnamese dishes, and his mom some Italian. There were little thin pancakes wrapped around shrimp and lemongrass, a sweet pudding made with ricotta cheese, and shell-shaped cookies covered in chocolate. It was a wonder no one in his family was fat.

"What'd you tell your dad?" I asked Tony.

"I told him we were sleeping over up here above the store."

"He didn't mind?"

"It's practically across the hall." Tony gestured out the window. "What'd you tell your folks?"

"That you and I were having a sleepover and just that. I knew they'd figure it was at your place."

"What if they call?"

"They probably won't, but if they do, I'm in big trouble. Well, at least your dad knows where we are. In case . . ."

" 'In case . . .' " Tony repeated.

"Maybe we should —"

"You done with this?" Tony interrupted. I nodded, stuffed. He closed up the containers. "We can eat again later," he said.

We laid our sleeping bags out next to each other on the floor.

"Did you read in yesterday's paper about the guy who was digging up bodies in the cemetery? He was cutting out the eyes and selling them to these cult people who use them in spells," Tony offered.

"When we were little," I reminded him, "your dad used to tell us that story about the guy who was missing his toe —"

96

"Yeah, and he'd creep around the room, howling, 'Who stole my toe?' and then suddenly grab one of us." Tony laughed. Then both of us stopped, frozen.

A wind picked up out of nowhere. They say that Chicago is the windy city, but Cleveland's got to be a close second. Maybe the wind was there all along, but talking about dug-up bodies and stolen toes made us aware of it. Soon, a tree limb started tapping away at the window. The next thing we heard was the long sad creak of the downstairs door sliding quietly, quietly open.

We froze.

Then Tony ran to the kitchen and turned off the light, so the only illumination came from the street-lights.

It seemed to take an hour for the door to creak closed. Then, we listened as the heaviest footsteps in the world slowly made their way — *thud, thud, thud* — up the stairs. At the top, we heard the heavy breathing, a man's breathing, a loud groan, then a squeak as the doorknob twisted. More light came in as the door swung slowly open, creaking like the one below, only louder.

A huge man appeared in the doorway. He stood with his legs and arms stiffly apart, like Frankenstein. He didn't seem to see us. He grunted, then lumbered heavily in. I knew then that, in the last moments of your life, you don't think of big things, but small things. I thought about when my dad brought in the angelfish and we got donuts and coffee and set up our chairs in front of the aquarium and watched the ripple of his fins as he moved in the water. My mom talked about how, when she was little, she believed angels were contained in snowflakes and that their lives on earth were as long or as short as the snow stayed frozen. My dad said he was taught that angels were strangers who helped you out when you were in a jam—when your car was broken down or when you needed help carrying something really heavy—and then they just disappeared. *Anyone* could be an angel, my dad said, so you had to be nice to everyone. "Even a fish," I joked, and we had all laughed.

And I thought about when Sharon and I were walking on the cold, silent streets, and she asked me if I felt like an actor.

The man tripped, bumped into a chair, cursed, then stood towering over us.

I closed my eyes tightly and waited for . . . I didn't know what: to be clobbered, murdered, arrested. In a squeaky little voice, I heard Tony mumble, "Holy cow!"

chapter 15

"They're here, all right!" Frankenstein said loudly. "But why all the lights are out is beyond me."

I opened my eyes and looked up at the towering figure. His voice seemed familiar, but I didn't really know why. I heard lighter steps skitter to the kitchen. The light went on, and I looked at the familiar face.

"Thanks, Loafer." Sharon handed him several twenty-dollar bills.

"I don't like it." Loafer shoved the bills into his pocket. "I don't trust 'em." He motioned to us.

Tony gaped back and forth between Loafer and Sharon. He looked like he was in some spooky movie and couldn't find his way out.

"It's Sharon's chauffeur."

"Someone's banging a drum in my chest." He gulped.

"Listen, I can handle myself with these two. Besides"—Sharon pulled a small black box out of her backpack—"I have my cell phone. If I need you, I'll call."

"I don't know."

"Loafer." She tapped her foot. "I've got about a million ways to blackmail you."

"Who cares?" Loafer said, but in a friendly way. "You two better be gentlemen."

"Are you inferring that we would have romantic interest in *that*?" Tony pointed to Sharon. Sharon stuck out her tongue.

"We'll behave," I said to Loafer, then blushed because I realized what we were doing tonight was about as far from behaving as I'd ever gotten.

"Well, all right, but I'm gonna park outside."

"Oh, go back to bed," Sharon ordered. "We'll be fine."

Loafer backed slowly out of the room. His long mustache made him look like a giant walrus.

Sharon had brought three pieces of luggage. It was like she was going on a European vacation rather than just camping out for the night. She unpacked her sleeping bag, clothes, a radio, a reading lamp, a comb, a brush, a mirror, some books, and a bunch of other stuff.

"You owe me a dollar," I whispered to Tony.

"I guess." He sighed.

"Why?" Sharon perked right up.

"Nothing," I said.

"We had a bet going . . . on whether you would chicken out," Tony said.

"How uncouth." For a minute I thought she wasn't going to talk to us anymore. She pulled her sleeping bag across to the other side of the room.

"We were getting bored," I offered.

"Well, what did you bet, Aaron?"

"That you would come."

"Well, if you bet on me, I guess it's okay."

Of course, at that, Tony made about a million faces behind her back, but I pretended I didn't see them (acting again).

"What's all this mess?" She stared into the containers of food. I could tell she was hungry.

"Dinner," I said. "There's plenty left over for you."

"From *your* restaurant?" She pointed to Tony.

"The very best."

"No, thank you. I don't need food poisoning tonight."

"Don't knock it if you haven't tried it," Tony said.

"I suppose you're right." She reached in and pulled out one of the little pancakes wrapped around lemongrass and shrimp. She ate it in a few little bites.

"Not bad, I guess," she said, "for fast food."

"What do you mean, *'fast food'*! Don't you know the difference between McDonald's and cuisine?" Tony jumped up, and the two of them started yelling at each other. It took me about five minutes before I could calm them down.

"This is supposed to be a stakeout!" I pulled them apart. "Not a riot!"

"Fine." Sharon sat down.

"Can we keep it to a whisper?" I begged.

"He started it."

"I did not!"

Sharon loaded up a plate of food and sat on her side of the room, glaring.

"Hey, Aaron, you know why Molly Pringle's hair is green?" I knew better than to ask why, but it didn't matter. Tony made a gesture, wiping his hand from his nose up into his hair.

"Ewww," Sharon said. "I am *trying* to eat."

"But you don't even *like* the food!" Tony shouted. I could see they were going to start yelling again.

Sharon had worked her way to the ricotta pudding. She held the spoon in midair. "Actually," she admitted, "it's fantastic!"

Tony stumbled back. "Really?"

"It's great. I have to tell you." She shoved another bite into her mouth. "I've never tasted anything this good. No kidding. And I eat at a lot of fancy restaurants."

"Well, my parents made a really special meal tonight."

Sharon pulled her sleeping bag closer to us.

I couldn't believe it: a truce.

"Did you hear about that guy who was selling eyeballs to witches and stuff?" Sharon munched on a cookie.

"Yeah!" Tony got all excited. "They said he carved them out with a *spoon*!"

"I read one report that said he actually ate them!"

The two of them went on and on together about murderers and dismembered corpses. I lay back on my sleeping bag and tried to count the square tiles of the ceiling, but it was too dark. I closed my eyes and tried to imagine going through my nightly rituals. I pictured myself setting up my room, just so, before climbing into bed

(I can't sleep until the room is tidy), and watching the elm branches sway outside my window.

"Hey!" Tony tapped me. "Are you asleep?"

I sat up. My eyes felt like they were being propped open by toothpicks. "No. Just resting."

"You guys get your valentines yet?" Sharon asked.

"Nah," Tony said.

"Are you going to get me a special valentine, Aaron?" Sharon piped up.

Boy, did I wish she wouldn't say stuff like that. Tony could barely contain his guffaws.

"My mom always picks them out of some wildlife catalog." I yawned. "Everyone will get a lion, a zebra, or a giraffe."

"Your mom picks out your valentines?" Sharon sounded shocked.

"Sure."

"Mine, too," Tony admitted. "But she knows better than to get me anything but sports ones."

"Even for the girls?" Sharon asked.

"Sure. I'm gonna get plenty of Little Mermaids and Hello Kitties from the girls. My mom puts in those little heart candies with messages on them, too."

"Last year"—Sharon glared at me—"David Campbell picked out all of his BE MINE hearts and gave them to me in a Dixie cup."

"Whooo-hoo." Tony rolled his eyes. "The height of romance. Hey, remember in second grade, when Roger Somner put those little plastic barfs in all the girls' valentines?"

"Oh yeah!" Sharon laughed.

"That was hilarious!"

"He got suspended for a day."

"That's right. I wonder where he got those. Remember the joke shop that used to be on this block, Aaron?"

I was trying hard to look awake. "Uh-huh."

"And in third grade," Sharon offered, "Aaron drew the valentines himself."

"That's right!" Tony said. "Those were amazing."

"Oh yeah. I drew unicorns."

"That must've taken you forever. They were so detailed."

"I still have mine," Sharon said.

"Hey, have we been in class together since second grade?" Tony asked.

"Since first! In Mr. Migrant's class. Now, he was a character."

Tony and Sharon chattered like they were long-lost friends. They both seemed to remember every gross thing that had happened to us over the last five years. If a kid had barfed on the floor or peed his pants or put a smashed frog in the teacher's lunch box, they recalled it and talked about it in excruciating detail.

With Sharon's reading light and their voices, the room lost its spooky feel. The wind turned into rain, which got heavier and heavier, like my eyelids. I tried to hold on to my thoughts, to pay attention to the exchange of jokes and stories, the voices, the light on the red walls, but the rain and sleepiness melted them like chalk drawings on a sidewalk.

chapter 16

Sometimes I get why my dad likes to sleep so much. I woke up from a dream where I was riding on a camel through this amazing desert. The sand was pale gold. The camel's movement rocked me like I was on a boat. In front of me, on another camel, was Sharon Trout. She was wearing a veil that had emeralds and rubies at the top of it, like a little crown. Even in my dream, she was rich.

I tried to come out of the dream slowly, but a foul odor brought me quickly to my senses. Tony Wong had turned around in his sleep, and his Limburger cheese feet were right in my face.

I rolled away from him. The rain had stopped. The morning light was so bright, it was as if someone were spraying it in with a hose.

My eyes took in my new home. In the corner, on the ceiling, a brown spot spread where water had accumulated from the rain. A leaky roof. Great!

I closed my eyes and started to doze. I could hear Sharon's light, dainty breathing and Tony's thick breathing. It took me a second to realize that there was a third sound: a thick wheezing noise, like the breath of an asthmatic who's just run a marathon in the smog.

I sat bolt upright.

A man was bent over the container where Ronald Reagan had been kept. From behind, I could see wrinkled white trousers, a tight navy blazer, and beat-up red Converse high-tops.

I could tell he was old by the slowness of his movement. I could practically hear his muscles creak.

"I hope it wasn't *I* who woke you." He turned around.

His face was bright cherry red, like he'd been in the sun for about fifty years. He pulled off his cap—the cap we'd found—and smoothed away at a few snow white hairs on his forehead. I looked at his jacket, wondering if he "packed a gun," as Tony would say, but it was hard to believe he would *pack* anything. He looked like someone's grandpa.

Sharon stirred. She sat up slowly and opened her eyes. I could tell she didn't like what she saw, because, at the sight of the old man, she opened her mouth like she was going to scream.

"Sharon, wait," I urged.

"I should introduce myself," the man apologized. "Captain Clarence Blue. Curator of nautical museums, collector of navigational tools and carved wooden pipes, carpenter — before the arthritis, gymnast, boxer, bricklayer, plumber, baker, artist, brewmaster, recovered alcoholic, goat-cheese-producing farmer, carnie, dentist without portfolio, zoologist, proprietor, botanist, and, above all, sea captain extraordinaire." He tipped his cap to Sharon.

"Sharon Trout." She stuck out a shaky hand. "Girl extraordinaire."

"I have no doubt." He shook her hand and turned to me.

"Aaron," I offered.

"So good to meet you."

Tony let out a snore and rolled over. "And that's Tony," Sharon said. "You're seeing him at his best."

"I enjoy the sentiment, Miss Trout, but don't believe a word of it. I have seen that young man play baseball, from this very window, and he is an athlete—"

Tony rolled over and grabbed a pillow. "Mommy," he said.

"And now that we've had the introductions, dear children, would you please tell me, what have you done with my pets?"

"*Your* pets?" Sharon burst out. "Do you know who this is?"

"Aaron," the captain said. "Didn't catch the last name."

"Aaron *Betts*," Sharon replied.

"Betts. Betts. Betts? Oh, I see. I see." He rubbed his red shiny head. "And here I thought you were the intruders, the interlopers, the interceders, when indeed you'll be the interrogators. Then you . . ." He pointed to me, and his mood changed instantly from sad to happy. "You are the young man whose drawings I've so much admired in the seed room."

It took me a second to figure out what he was talking about. But then I remembered. My animal sketches are in a big pile on a shelf in the storeroom.

"How did you get into the storeroom?" I asked.

"Ah." He walked to a door, which I'd assumed was a closet, and opened it. "This door, of course, goes straight to the storeroom."

"But there's no door down there."

"There is. There is. Of course, there is. Although you keep so many boxes in front of it, it's really quite a task to get in and out."

"Where the shelves are?" I asked.

"Precisely."

"Not now, Mom!" Tony mumbled in his sleep. "The ornaments are still on the tree."

"I brought the animals back to the shop," I finally answered his question.

"Oh, I am sorry. You see, I only borrowed them for a while to keep me company and to cheer up a precious friend of mine who visits on occasion."

Bits of dust floated in the bright light. There was something teasing my mind, but I couldn't get to it.

"Well, you seemed to take good care of them," Sharon said, politely.

"Indeed I did, Miss Trout. Indeed I did."

"You can call me Sharon. I've never really liked my last name much."

"It's perfectly elegant." He smiled. "And certainly my favorite fish to eat."

Then it popped into my mind. The man Bertha was yelling to when we drove by. And her face as she finished every tale! Captain. That was what she said. Captain. "Do you know Bertha?" I asked.

"Do I know Bertha?" The little cap had slipped to one side of his head. He looked out the window to where the melted snow dripped off the eaves onto the street. "Oh yes, I know the Bertha of whom you speak, but her name isn't Bertha."

"It isn't?" If there was one thing Bertha seemed sure of, it was her name.

"Her name is Katherine Hamilton Hart, and she is the woman I've loved for the larger part of my seventy-odd years." He took off his cap. The top of his head was shiny. "Oh, you wouldn't imagine the beauty and grace of Katherine Hamilton when I met her. How the mighty are fallen . . ."

"Are you married?" Sharon asked.

The cap went straight over his heart. He reminded me of one of those old-fashioned actors. His gestures were grand, out of place in the small apartment.

"That, dear, near Sharon, is a very long story."

chapter 17

The Captain pulled up an old box. On the side of it, in Mom's writing, it read, MOM AND DAD — MEMORABILIA. It occurred to me then that the Captain was probably my mom's parents' age if they hadn't driven off to Florida one foggy morning only to be run off the road by a truck.

"I'm an ornithologist—I think I forgot to mention that." He sat on the box. "A bird aficionado, affectionato. I met Katherine when she was married to her first husband, Seagram Hart, the third—only his name shouldn't have been Hart, because he didn't have one. Oh, he had a ticker all right, a ticker tocker like a clocker. No doubt it told perfect and accurate time, but oh, was he heartless. Katherine had been an accomplished flautist—that's one who plays the flute—"

"*I* play the viola," Sharon piped up.

"Wonderful. We must listen sometime."

"What next?" I asked. I wished Sharon wouldn't interrupt.

"What next?" He seemed lost in thought. "What next?"

"She played the flute . . ." I prompted.

"Yes. And she put all her love—the love that her husband rejected—into her music, her garden, and her birds. She had money—did she ever. She went from a wealthy, painful childhood into a wealthy, empty marriage. To fill her sad hours, she raised rare birds."

"How did you meet her?" Sharon asked.

"She hired me to build an aviary. This was not to be just an ordinary aviary, a big cage. This was to be . . . what should I call it? A work of art, a habitat of masterful proportions. It was"—he wiped his eyes and gazed out the window; as if on cue, two sparrows flew onto the phone wire—"exquisite, ethereal, wonderful! The finest aviary ever built."

Tony turned again and kicked the covers.

"Go on," Sharon urged.

114

"Every morning, I toiled on that aviary, and Katherine played the flute. In the afternoons, we had tea together and talked and talked for hours. Oh, the things we talked about: botany, music, God, books! We both loved Dickens, the way the world was divided in his books into good and evil people, which is how, in reality, life is. It took twice as long to complete the job as I had planned. Then one sad day, the aviary was completed. We had attempted just about everything that could be added. Her husband was pressuring me — us — to finish. We had our last day together: a little ceremony, a celebration, a coronation, a commemoration. I presented her with the key to the beautiful gold aviary lock inlaid with mother-of-pearl. She paid me with a profusely large check. I started to leave but turned back. Do you know what she had done?"

"What?" Sharon asked.

"What?" I echoed.

"She had locked herself into the aviary. 'I'm in a cage,' she said. 'It may be beautiful. It may be fancy . . .' "

Again, he gazed out the window. Other birds had joined the parade on the phone line. There were blackbirds, pigeons, and a couple of crows. It seemed like they were listening.

The Captain pointed at them. "Happy as clams, aren't they? Why do people say that? Clams aren't really happy, just secure. Where was I?"

"She locked herself in!" we exclaimed.

"We ran away together." He smiled. "We moved to Nova Scotia, where I painted houses, mended fences, and she worked as a children's librarian."

"The nursery rhymes!" I said.

"Oh, she loved all those stories and rhymes. See, she could never have children, and that was her way of compensating, completing."

"What about her husband?" Sharon asked.

"He tried to find us, and we were very afraid he would. You see, he was a powerful man. There was no telling what he would've done. Years passed. We figured he'd meet someone else, some other unfortunate soul, and divorce Katherine, the deserting wife, you know. But come to find out, he never did. I like to imagine that in some part of his dead heart, he knew what he'd lost." The Captain sighed. "We had thirty-five wonderful, happy years together, the first happy years of her life. I'd always been a drifter before, but when I met Katherine, I settled down. I never went to sea again, never left her side except to earn our meager bread."

"And did she mind?" Sharon asked.

"Mind what?"

Sharon blushed. "Not being . . . you know, rich?"

"Not a scoop, not a Hula-Hoop, not a Froot Loop. Because, you see, she was happy."

"But why does she think her name is Bertha?" I asked.

Captain Blue tapped his shiny forehead. "Thirty-five years and sharp as a whip. But then, all of a sudden, she began to do strange things. She would mix up the words in her nursery rhymes and shelve the books in the wrong places. The library had to let her go. At home, she'd put the hats in the oven and the pots and pans on the hat rack. She'd disappear and I'd chase after her, but it got to the point where she didn't know who I was."

"Tragic," Sharon gasped.

"Yes. It is. For me. For her? She still seems happy. I think that shedding the weight of the past, her childhood, the heartless Mr. Hart . . . Oh, you can be trapped by the past, as surely as your names are Sharon and Aaron, or even if they were Baron and Karen."

"Where is she?" I asked.

The Captain jolted suddenly and stood up. It was as if I had pulled him out of the past with my question. "I must go!" he said. "I always collect her on Monday mornings, and we come and see . . ." He looked around the room. "Oh . . . the pets."

"But where does she live now? And what happened to her?" I wanted to know.

"Thirty-five years," he said, "and we lived together in Canada, but then my work dropped off. Katherine's problems became worse. There were many expensive visits to doctors. I got an offer on a job here in Cleveland, and for a while we had a small apartment, but then we had to move ourselves into 'retirement housing,' subsidized by the state. That's a fancy way of saying an old people's home. Old . . ." He spit out the word. "Nothing old about Katherine and me. Or just a few things," he admitted. "What's worse, because we weren't married, we had to live in separate wings. That is where this apartment comes in."

"Did you *live* here?" Sharon whispered.

"No, but we came here on occasion. The pets amused her greatly, made her feel like she was at home. We'd always had lots of pets."

"So where is she now — the apartment?"

"I'm afraid not. Just last week, I became persuaded to check her into a different kind of facility, one that would see to her safety and care. It's called Memory Home. It's for people who don't remember. So you see, we use this apartment less and less. Sadly. She's allowed outings only twice a week at Memory Home. Today is the day."

"Why don't you bring her to the pet store?" Sharon volunteered.

The Captain nodded to me. "I don't think your parents would like that. I mean, she does get rather loud when she's excited. And when they find out I've been intruding and interloping in their apartment, thieving and borrowing their creatures, they'll have me thrown in jail."

"They won't!" I said. "I mean, I don't *think* they will if you explain."

"I'll do it!" he decided. "I'll bring Katherine here this afternoon."

Tony twitched and kicked his legs. He reminded me of a sleeping dog, dreaming of chasing rabbits.

The Captain adjusted his cap. "I must fly!" he said. "Thank you, children, for listening to my story."

"You *will* come back?" I asked.

"As sure as God made little apples," he offered, "and strawberries, peaches, artichokes, and cinnamon buns."

He left. We listened to his light steps go down the stairs.

"Wow," Sharon said.

"Double wow!" I echoed.

"I'm sorry I'll miss that."

"Why?" I felt truly disappointed.

"My mom's coming back this morning."

"Really?"

"Uh-huh."

"Well, can't you just slip out for a little while?"

"She'll want me to spend every second with her for a week or two, until her conscience is eased."

"I'm sure it's just 'cause she's missed you. I mean . . . you're a lot of fun."

"Really?" She smiled.

But I didn't get to answer. Tony rolled over onto his back, groaned, then sat up slowly. "Did I miss anything?"

chapter 18

I guess I didn't believe that the Captain would come back, because when he walked in the door, I felt a rush of excitement. It was the way I felt once when my drawing won first prize in the school art show. My excitement turned to disappointment, though; Bertha wasn't with him.

"May I help you?" Dad rushed to meet the Captain. Usually my dad just sits on his stool until the customers ask him something. I wondered if his conversations with Mom had made him turn on the salesmanship.

"Captain Clarence Blue." The Captain extended his hand. "Very pleased to meet you."

"Birds, reptiles, or mammals?" Dad gestured to our various departments. "Or an aquarium, perhaps?"

"Well, all of them, as far as I'm concerned, but I'm afraid they don't allow pets where I live."

"Oh."

"Dad," I interrupted, "Mr. Blue is sort of married to Bertha . . . I mean, Katherine."

" 'Sort of'?" Dad asked.

"I found the birdseed." Mom came in. "But it's opened."

"Mom, this is Captain Blue."

"Hello." Mom wiped her hand on her pants and extended it.

"He's sort of married to Bertha," Dad explained.

"Oh, your little friend from the garden?"

My friend could be a ten-foot-tall linebacker and Mom would call him my "little friend."

"Uh-huh," I replied.

"Only her real name, her true name, is Katherine," the Captain explained.

"How is she?" Mom asked. Of my parents, she is definitely the one with the social skills.

"Oh, fine and not so fine. That is, I promised this young man that I would bring her in today, but I'm afraid I must disappoint. You see my wife, uh, Katherine, has had a slight turn for the worse." He tapped his head. "Mentally, that is. The doctor at Memory Home is now restricting her from leaving the premises. He's an old friend of ours, this doctor. I'm afraid I must obey his instructions."

"I'm sorry," Mom said.

"But all is not lost!" he explained. "Because if we can't bring Bertha — as you call her — to the boy, we will bring the boy to Bertha!"

"You mean you want Aaron to visit her?" Dad asked, sniffing out an outing.

"Indeed," the Captain said, "this very day."

"Can I?" I asked.

"If your father goes with you."

"Then it's all settled." The Captain grinned. "Katherine will be so happy to see her young friend. And now . . . I have a confession to make."

chapter 19

Luckily for me, Captain Blue left out the part about Sharon, Tony, and me being there to "capture" him. He talked about "squatting" in the apartment and "borrowing" the pets to amuse Bertha.

Much to my relief, my parents didn't rush for the police or get mad at him. Dad checked out the secret door, something he'd forgotten about years ago. Mom sighed and explained to the Captain that she wouldn't even mind his *staying* there, except we would be moving there ourselves. Business wasn't at its best, she understated. She'd start teaching in the spring, too.

Mom glanced at me uneasily as she said all this, but I only shrugged. It wasn't like she was telling me something I didn't already know. *At least they aren't selling the shop.* Yet.

On the drive over, my dad and the Captain talked non-stop.

Dad told his favorite story: "I was born in that pet shop, in the aisle between reptiles and rodents. It was snowing that day, and my dad couldn't find a cab. In those days, a retired doctor lived in the building. He finally came down and delivered me."

"What an exciting entrance," the Captain exclaimed.

"Of course, my parents closed up shop that day. It's the only day we've ever been closed aside from holidays."

"It's a grand shop," the Captain added. "Maybe you can do more advertising."

"We've tried everything," Dad admitted.

"Take a left at that light. Then go past the old brewery."

"When I was a teenager," Dad said, "there was a dance at that old brewery, but all they served *us* was root beer."

"My favorite beverage."

Between the car heater and their voices, I started to doze off. Toddy, whom we brought along to cheer up Bertha, kept me awake, though, by letting out an occasional squawk.

"We're almost there," the Captain said.

I tried to imagine Bertha's new home.

Would it be a mansion on a sprawling green lawn, or a set of small buildings like a roadside motel? Would nurses be rushing around, like in a hospital?

Memory Home. I pictured a bunch of old people watching home movies together. They'd be passing popcorn and saying, "This is when Martha and I caught a fish at the lake," or, "This is my son's wedding." But I knew that wasn't it. It wasn't a place where people came to remember. It was where they were *put* when they forgot.

"Here we are," the Captain exclaimed. My dad pulled into a parking space.

The building was the same gray color as the sidewalk. It had a tattered green awning, like the kind you see on chic restaurants where people sit on the sidewalk drinking coffee. I looked up and counted from the top: ten stories down, twenty windows across.

A brass plaque on the bottom floor was engraved with black letters: MEMORY HOME. A couple of nurses leaned against the building, smoking cigarettes and laughing. One of them was short and chubby. The other was tall with a long neck, which she craned toward us, like a giraffe reaching for leaves from a high tree.

"They call such a place as this a *rest home*, but don't you believe it, because the likes of them"— the Captain pointed to the nurses—"won't give you a minute's rest. It's time for a pill or a change of sheets or a blood pressure check or a poke with a needle."

As if they knew we were discussing them, the nurses stopped talking and stared at us.

We stepped into a sort of lobby. Immediately, a lady in a lime green suit came rushing over. "You can't bring that *thing* in here." She pointed at Toddy. The woman was a dead ringer for a Shar-Pei, the exotic dog whose skin hangs in all kinds of folds around its face. Shar-Peis are cute. The lady was not.

"May I speak to Dr. Springer?" the Captain asked politely. "I think he'll make an exception."

"You may speak to whomever you please, but the bird can wait outside!"

The Captain turned to us. "Just a minute." He walked over to a desk where a nurse was looking through some papers. When she saw him, she lit right up and launched into a conversation.

Dad leaned over and whispered in my ear. "Smells like prune soup in here."

"Yeah," I agreed. The place did not excite my appetite. It smelled like the windows were opened about once every fifty years. There was bright gold carpeting and a big torn tweedy-looking couch. A line of wooden chairs stood in a row.

The Shar-Pei lady still glared at us while the Captain shot the breeze with the nurse. When Toddy let out a squawk, the lady shook her head so hard that the folds in her neck wobbled back and forth.

"Don't carry on, Toddy," Dad scolded. "You'll get us thrown out on our ears. Say 'Good morning, ma'am. Good morning.'"

Toddy gave my dad a dirty look. I'll bet he wished he were with Mom.

Finally, the nurse came over with the Captain. "I've spoken to Dr. Springer," she said to the first lady. "He feels that it will be therapeutic for Mrs. Hart to see the bird." She said to us, "Come this way."

We followed the nurse to a locked door. "These are my friends, the Bettses," the Captain told her.

The nurse smiled. "Pleased to meet you." She punched a code on a panel in the door, and it opened. "You know the way, Captain. No funny business."

"You have my word."

Ahead of us was a long white hall. The nurse closed the door and left us. It occurred to me that we were now locked inside.

"What did she mean, 'no funny business'?" Dad asked.

"Oh, I've already tried to spring Katherine once. Against doctor's orders."

"You mean, take her out?" I asked.

"Yes. I'm not much for rules, I'm afraid."

As we walked down the hall, I started hearing voices. It reminded me of all the times I thought I heard something upstairs. There was a woman's voice whispering something about the Civil War, and a man's voice reciting what seemed to be a poem about the ocean. I heard a television program on somewhere. It sounded like Oprah Winfrey. When a woman said that she lost "half of herself" in weight, the audience applauded loudly.

Finally, at the end of the hall, the Captain stopped and tapped on a door. There was no answer, so he pushed it open.

The room was dimly lit, like a motel room before you've turned on the lights. There was a single bed made up with white sheets, a white dresser, and a small bedside table.

Bertha sat on a wooden chair by the window. Her arms were resting on the sill, and her face was pressed against the glass.

I was glad to see that she had a view, at least. There was a small courtyard, with benches and a big tree.

"Look who's here," the Captain said softly.

Bertha turned and looked straight at me. "Captain," she said, "I've got a new one! Mary, Mary, quite contrary, where did my garden go? Be fast. Be slow. Beware of Miss Muffet eating her bagel and cream cheese. My name is Bertha."

I'd always felt her rhymes had a code, and this one was pretty clear.

"Hi, Bertha," I whispered, and all of a sudden I felt like crying, because this was it. Change. I wouldn't see her in the garden ever again. And I wouldn't even hear her soft voice up in the attic, because she would be here from now on. And you had to punch in a secret code to even open the door.

"So, you've found her!" Dad said happily, swinging Toddy's cage up onto the table.

"And here's another friend, dear," the Captain said. "With feathers."

Toddy moved his head in jerky little movements until his eyes fixed on Bertha. Then he opened his mouth and let out a squawk.

Bertha dashed over and peered into the cage.

"Toddy, mind your manners," Dad admonished.

Toddy puffed himself up and cocked his head. He examined Bertha as if *she* were the animal in the cage.

A woman down the hall yelled loudly for persimmons. The guests on Oprah Winfrey applauded. The Captain pulled over Bertha's chair, and she sat in front of Toddy's cage.

"Good morning, birdy," Bertha cried. "Good morning!"

"Good morning, ma'am," Toddy said. "Good morning. Good morning."

"He spoke!" Dad exclaimed.

Bertha clapped her hands together. "Jack be nimble, Jack be quick. Jack up the car. Hijack. Jackknife. Jack-of-all-trades. My name is Bertha."

"Hi, Jack! Hi, Jack!" Toddy repeated.

"What a fine specimen," the Captain gestured at Toddy. "Isn't he a fine specimen, Bertha?"

"Fine, Captain. Fine," Bertha agreed.

"Can she keep him?" I asked.

"Oh, Aaron, I doubt that they'd let her keep such a noisy bird, or any bird at all."

"Dad, even that guy who was in prison on Alcatraz got to have canaries!"

"Well, maybe they'd let her have a finch or something."

"And I could come over and clean the cage," I volunteered.

"We shall ask the doctor!" the Captain said.

"Hi, Jack!" Toddy shouted, overjoyed to have finally found his voice.

"Oh, she's happy, she is. Katherine is happy today!" The Captain put his arm around Bertha. "It's a shame that your little friend couldn't be with us this afternoon, Aaron. We'd have a regular party."

Bertha pressed her face right up to the bars of Toddy's cage. The Captain pulled out some cards and dealt a hand to my dad.

"There was an old woman who lived in a sock on the block," Bertha began. Toddy was a very receptive audience.

I looked out the window at the small courtyard. Aside from the big tree in the middle, the whole thing was brick. There wasn't any room for a garden.

I wondered if Bertha felt the difference between the open space of the lot and the closed space of the courtyard and her room. She was safer, I guess, but it seemed like a pretty big tradeoff.

"Come play a hand, Aaron," the Captain urged.

I sat next to my dad on the bed.

I thought about how all of this was a result of Sharon's gutsy plan, and how sorry I was that she wasn't there to meet Bertha. But I knew there'd be another time.

I figured that on the way home, I'd get Dad to stop at the mall. There's a shop that sells cards and stuff like that. I'd buy Sharon one of those heart-shaped boxes of candy, and the best valentine I could find.